Bohumil Hrabal was born on 28 March, 1914, in Czechoslovakia. He studied law in Prague and completed his studies, but after 1939, during the German occupation, it was almost impossible for him to practise. Since then he has been employed as a clerk, railway lineman, train dispatcher, postman, labourer in a steel works and sceneshifter in a theatre. He wrote his first novel in 1963, but in 1968 several of his works were blacklisted, and today certain novels of his, like the widely praised I SERVED THE KING OF ENGLAND, can only be published abroad. Hrabal is also the author of the classic CLOSELY OBSERVED TRAINS, also published by Abacus.

Michael Heim is the translator, with Simon Karlinsky, of THE LETTERS OF ANTON CHEKHOV.

Also by Bohumil Hrabal in Abacus:

CLOSELY OBSERVED TRAINS

BOHUMIL HRABAL

The Death of
Mr Baltisberger

Translated from the Czech by Michael Henry Heim
Introduction translated from the Czech by
Kaca Polackova

This book was originally published in Czechoslovakia under the
title *Automa Svět* by Bohumil Hrabal by Mlada Fronta
First published in Great Britain by
Sphere Books Ltd in Abacus 1990

Copyright © Bohumil Hrabal 1966

Printed and bound in Great Britain by
Richard Clay Ltd, Bungay, Suffolk

ISBN 0 349 10158 2

Sphere Books Ltd
A Division of
Macdonald & Co (Publishers) Ltd
Orbit House, 1 New Fetter Lane, London EC4A 1AR
A member of Maxwell Macmillan Pergamon Publishing Corporation

Introduction

Reality is alcoholic.
MR. KYTKA

The occasional successes enjoyed by authors who write in one of the world's "minor" languages often have unfortunate consequences for writers who subsequently compose in that same language. Reviewers familiar only with "major" languages tend to create pigeonholes to use in classifying the entire diverse literature of that "minor" language. They fall back on oversimplification, to the general satisfaction of their readers, and to the trivial irritation of the author thus pigeonholed. This reflex often operates in such a way that any Czech writer displaying even the slightest sense of humor is classified as a successor to Jaroslav Hasek (*The Good Soldier Schweik*). But pasting the label "Schweik" (as encompassing all things Czech) across the entirety of Bohumil Hrabal's short stories—although he personally admires this Czech classic—would be only a little closer to the mark than describing William Faulkner as "Mark Twainian" because they both used folksy material.

There is yet another misconception, besides the Schweik comparison, that may attach itself to Hrabal, though this collection should do much to remedy it. The Academy Award-winning film *Closely Watched Trains* was a conventionalized restructuring of Hrabal's most conventional novella and the latter was itself an adaptation of a radically unconventional piece that Hrabal wrote in the early fifties entitled *Legend of Cain*. I am saying this not as a criticism, but rather as an attempt to indi-

v

cate that the true Hrabal, the one who did much in the sixties to change radically ideas about Czech literature, is to be found neither in Menzel's famous film, nor in the fact that Hrabal, like Hasek, likes to drink his beer in taverns (*because in every bar people say something nice* [*Prague Nativity*]). The true Hrabal, rather, can be found in these stories. Works of art, they are a synthesis of "high" or "low," and the influences that formed them extend far beyond the borders of the Prague periphery, or of Czech literature.

Of course, what we have here above all is urban folklore, filtered through the author's own experiences. Hrabal, born in 1914, graduated from Charles University with a doctorate in law, but the madhouse that was European history around the middle of this century brought its influence to bear, and so the only bar that the law school graduate Hrabal ever came close to was the one in any number of Prague's pubs.

His biography is what we in Europe used to think of as "American": a Jack-of-all-trades, he has been a traveling salesman, a steelworker, a dealer in scrap paper, a stagehand. He married a charming waitress who appears to have stepped right out of the story *The World Cafeteria*, and he stylized himself into the figure of a beer drinker who thinks like an intellectual but speaks in the language of the palavering populace. With the typical understatement of a writer subjected to an excess of critical attention, he refers to himself not as a writer but as a reporter, in the original sense of the word: a chronicler of beer-hall stories.

At one of our last joint meetings with readers in Czechoslovakia, in 1968, he complained, "I'm as good as done for. Those guys heard about the money I'm supposed to be raking in by putting their stories down on paper, and so now whenever I walk into a tavern, all I hear is 'Here he comes, the great writer! Wants to make another hundred thousand by just sitting around listening.' And they clam up and scowl in their beer. Yes, I'm done for."

Obviously, Hrabal is not done for, not by a long shot, and this story is just another example of his palavering. But we do find traces of folklore in his works, and the American reader needn't look far to see that its roots are deep in the same kind of soil in which the American tall stories of humorous exaggeration germinated. The old man, exploded twenty feet into the air with a quarter ton of flying excrement (*Palaverers*)—isn't he a not too distant cousin of Paul Bunyan, Davy Crockett, or Pecos Bill?

Yes, the sense of fun characterized by the Davy Crocketts has long since transcended the borders of the United States. Through silent film comedies—the forgotten art of the gag—it has come to join hands with jazz to make a noticeable mark on Czech art as far back as the twenties and to blend with the native folklore of the Prague urban milieu into an infrangible alloy. That is why Hrabal garnishes his stories with scenes from the early two-reelers of Charlie Chaplin, Buster Keaton, Lupino Lane. Take, for instance, the youth so extraordinarily absorbed in reading that he even takes a leak with his nose in a book; or the girl who breaks through a door panel with her head and knocks down a neighbor lady snooping at the keyhole; or the old geezer with a pot of sauerkraut in his hand, following the splendid butt of a shapely beauty down the street . . .

But there are other, unexpected clues to be found. The narration of Uncle Pepin (*The Death of Mr. Baltisberger*), who, incidentally, is based on Hrabal's real-life uncle of the same name, comes up with an element from classical American literary theory, stripped of the author's name and dropped a few notches to accommodate the needs of tavern yarn-spinners: [I] *consoled her with the thought that the poets say the most beau-*

tiful thing in the world is a dead beauty. Could it be that the shade of the radiant Lenore has found its way by some strange paths all the way to the selfsame tavern where the Good Soldier Schweik used to tell his tales about dog turds? Or was it perhaps imported by the erudite ex-stagehand, an admirer of Nelson Algren and William Faulkner? The novelette *Dancing Lessons for the Elderly and Advanced,* written in one book-long sentence, is a direct tribute to Faulkner.

There is no telling. So far, it could all be part of the genuine folklore experience, including the pair of naked caryatids who meet during a performance of *Troilus and Cressida.* And the common woman who reads Milton. For the fact is that we are reading of Prague, a city that is imbued with culture, in a nation whose nearly extinct language was artificially revived by a group of eighteenth- and ninteenth-century intellectuals using translations of Milton, Byron, and Shakespeare. And Poe—there are at least twenty different Czech translations of *The Raven.* But as we look further into Hrabal, we find ourselves in pure literature:

> . . . *she carried the hemisphere of the half-loaf of bread beside that black hair of hers and the white crust sketched her path in the darkness* . . . (*Romance*)
> . . . *the black propman's green skull emerged from the black velvet backdrop* . . . *then, as black velvet drapes were slipped open by the green skull suddenly as it had appeared, it slipped back into the deep purple darkness* . . . (*A Prague Nativity*)

Now we are close to Stephen Crane, both his impressionistic and his expressionistic planes. Which of course is not to say that the author of *Maggie* and *The Monster* was Hrabal's model, but rather that they both had one supremely important source of inspiration in common: the fine arts. The key to Crane's imagination is impressionism, the trend that launched modern art. The key to the imagination that is Hrabal's is the most durable scion of modern art's family tree: surrealism.

"I don't actually write," Hrabal used to say in his talks with readers. "I cut, and then glue the cut-outs together into collages." Sometimes he does it literally, without using his own words: *The Reader's Own Mortuary Ballad* (from the collection *Mortuary Ballads and Legends*) is in fact a literary collage, consisting of fragments chosen from letters of his readers without a single word added by the author. For the most part, however, they are collages made up of stories that, having passed through a sophisticated imagination, are glued together by a poetic text. But collages they remain: the forceful juxtaposition of images which—unlike Eisenstein's abstract montages—stress the concreteness of experience. Once removed from its accustomed contexts and placed by means of collages in the "liberated" context of dreams, palavering, and fantasy, this concreteness of experience becomes a reality more real than reality itself: a surreality. The juxtaposition of the dying Mr. Baltisberger (who, by the way, like the uncle was a concrete historical figure, a race driver actually killed while taking part in the Czechoslovak Grand Prix) and the irrelevant romantic bragging of Uncle Pepin; Little Eman and his odyssey through the taverns of Prague; the tipsy bride initiating her infidelity beside the almost still warm corpse of her lover-to-be's mistress, dead by her own hand—all these are collages. Such is Hrabal's fundamental narrative technique—and the basic method of the surrealists. A *reality* that *is alcoholic,* a manipulation of its concrete elements basically unrestricted by any sort of realism, Dali's "critical paranoia," André Breton's black humor.

When a work of art transcends the frontiers of its native land, it takes on a dual existence, as it were: its native existence, and its existence abroad. For the American reader, Hrabal will, I hope, appear as an interesting and original, perhaps an experimental, author of short stories. For Czechoslovakia, Hrabal was a revolution. In Czechoslovakia, Hrabal represents a category all his own.

Perhaps a brief excursion into the past would be appropriate. I met Hrabal under circumstances that sound like one of his own stories. In the early fifties I was an editor at a publishing house. One of my duties was delivering obsolete galley proofs to the scrap paper salvage center. The fellow in the patched overalls there examined my proofs with interest. Then he launched into a fluent discussion of literature; Breton's *Nadja,* I think, was his subject that day. He was just like Mr. Bedar, sorter of medicinal herbs, sitting in a pub, explaining modern art, or the youth with the frayed pants leg in *The World Cafeteria* defining *absolute graphics.* Later on this fellow and I would meet at the flat of poet and artist Jiří Kolář (known in the U.S.A. because there have been several exhibitions of his work in New York City), one of the typical centers of the Czech avant-garde, where we discussed abstract expressionism or whatever else was in the air in those days. And we also read aloud our verses and stories. It was at these sessions that I first heard *The Death of Mr. Baltisberger, The Legend of Cain, Jarmilka . . .*

But these were only private meetings; none of us was publishing anything. The literary taste of the times was different. It had to change before Hrabal's strange, unique tales could find their way to more readers than just the few, small groups of people interested in what was not quite in vogue—at least not with the publishers.

Eventually, the taste of the times did change. And with the

publication of *Lark on a String* in 1963 (after the first attempt by Hrabal to publish it in 1958 did not meet with success) the revolution came.

To understand why it was a revolution is, perhaps, not easy for an American reader, and an attempt to explain it would require something resembling a Ph.D. thesis. But perhaps a thesis is not really necessary. Maybe it is enough to bring to the reader's attention the story *The World Cafeteria*. In this wonderful story he will find a character who is of key significance: the artist of "absolute graphics." This character obviously has difficulties finding a gallery which is willing to exhibit his work. But the workers in the factory where he has a job like his unconventional art and see to it that he has an exhibition right at the factory, despite the protests of the functionary in charge of culture—a man who shares the taste of the times. The workers come into direct contact with modern art for the first time, through the efforts of their fellow employee. They do not know anything about the taste of the times, hence they cannot see why this man and this kind of weird picture should not be shown to the public. This story is, once again, an incident that actually happened to a friend of Hrabal's, Vladimir Boudnik, but at the same time it is also a metaphor for Hrabal's own struggle, and for the struggle of modern art against misunderstanding.

I hope that there is no misunderstanding now why Hrabal brought a revolutionary new quality to Czech prose during the late fifties and early sixties.

Bohumil Hrabal's last book to date, *This Town Is in the Collective Care of Its Citizens,* came out in 1967. Since that time nothing new has appeared from the pen of my old friend from the scrap paper salvage center and from the Kolář circle of avant-garde buffs. But there are rumors of several manuscripts being prepared for publication. Let's hope this rumor is true. Modern literature has not had too many writers like Hrabal, and their silence is something of a luxury that a "small" literature— that is, the literature of a small country—hardly can afford.

—DANIEL S. MIRITZ
Translated by Káča Poláčková

Handbook for the Apprentice Palaverer

I worship the sun in garden restaurants, I guzzle the moon mirrored in wet sidewalks, I walk along head high while my wife at home staggers around stone sober making a mess of things, a comical interpretation of Heraclitus' *panta rei* flows through my gullet and every beer hall on earth is a group of deer hooked together by the antlers of conversation, the large MEMENTO MORI exuding from things and human destinies is reason enough for drinking *sub specie aeternitatis,* and for that matter so are Prague's Olšany Cemeteries, Pankrác Jail, and Bartoloměj Street Police Station.

I am therefore a dogmatist of allergy in its fluid state, the theories of rod and reel are my motive force, I am a frightened human scream that falls apart at the touch of a snowflake, I am always rushing around so that I can work two or three hours a day of inactive dreaming into my schedule, because I know all too well that life flows by like a deck of cards being shuffled and that I would be much better off if I were laundered and folded away in a handkerchief somewhere, I sometimes try to look as though I had hopes of breaking the bank when I know damn well I will wind up with shit, that the whole shooting match began with a drop of semen and ends with a burst of fire, a beautiful end from beautiful beginnings, for a pretty face we make love to jolly old crone Death.

I water flowers when it rains, in sultry July I pull my December sled behind me, to keep cool on hot summer days I drink up the money I put aside for the coal to keep me warm in winter, it makes me nervous to think how unnervous people are about how short life is and how little time there is for going wild and getting drunk as long as there is time, I do not treat my morning hangover like a sample possessing no commercial value, I treat it as if it possessed the absolute value of poetic trauma with a touch of discord, which should be savored like a sacred gallbladder attack, I am a leafy tree full of sharp, smiling eyes in a constant state of grace and coupled axles of fortunes and misfortunes, how fine to see young shoots sprout from an old trunk, how fine to hear the laughter of newborn leaves on the youngest shoots,

my climate is the fickle weather of April, a spotted table-cloth my banner, in its rippling shadow I experience not only euphoria but also the downward path and resurrection, a dull ache in the nape of my neck, a terrible tremor in my hands, hands from which I bite out the splinters and other remains of the previous night's revelry, every morning I am amazed to find myself alive, I am always putting it off just so I can keep going long enough to go mad in my own way, I do not see myself as a rosary but as a broken chain of laughter, the most fragile bead determines the limits of my prodigal imagination, something in me has been castrated, something that both exists here and now and is retreating to the past, so as to be catapulted arclike into a future that keeps shrinking away from my hungry lips and eyes, which then makes me squint and look at things with the double vision of Icelandic limestone, today is yesterday and the day before yesterday is the day after tomorrow,

I am therefore a manufacturer of hurried, synthetic judgments, a fancier and connoisseur of adulterated space, I consider senility and dementia as well as the babble of infants to be the root of possible discoveries, with play and playfulness I change this vale of tears into laughter, I exorcise reality, but she does not always give me a sign, I am a shy deer in the clearing of brazen anticipation, I am the solid bell of imbecility cracked by the lightning of knowledge, my objectivity acquires extreme subjectivity, which I consider an accretion of nature and the social sciences, I am a negative genius, a poacher in the meadows of language, I am a game warden of comic inspiration, a tried and true ranger in the fields of the anonymous anecdote, a murderer of good ideas, a keeper of the questionable fish tanks of spontaneity, an eternal fan of and dabbler in debility and pornography, a hero of thinking thoughtlessness, a hurried and premature Knight of the Cross of Parallel Lines who hungers for a slice of bread buttered with infinity and thirsts for a stein of the cream of eternity now, right now, and never again, in other words, never, I find the charm of the apostolic writings to be the false interpretation of Christ's words, my finery is Brussels lace dipped in epileptic saliva and dangerous drift ice along the banks of a winter stream, I am depression, dejection, and low spirits, a running start for knocking my head against the wall, I keep putting off trying to find out if it is possible to live any other way than I have lived until now, I am a neurasthenic in excellent health, an insomniac who can sleep soundly only in a tram and therefore never gets off until the last stop,

I am the great present of small expectations and great expected wrecks and wrong notes, the horizons on my own grotesque horizon glimmer with minor provocations and miniature scandals, as a result I am a clown, an animator, a storyteller, and private tutor as well as informer, poison-pen pal, I regard worthless news items as possible preambles to my constitution, which I constantly alter, which I can never complete, I see gigantic constructions in the roughest of sketches, even when they are no more than rickety old child-sized coffins, I am a man growing old but pregnant with youth, my facial expression and words form the mobile grammar of my inner slang, within a half hour a warm plate of meat and a glass of cold lager can prove to me the transubstantiation of matter into good mood, cheap metamorphosis, the world's first miracle, a hand on a friendly shoulder is the knob that opens the door to bliss, in which each love object is the center of a garden of paradise, the heart of nature is an accessible state of *bodhi* in which it is possible to love a rebellious and hardheaded vagina wrapped in the most beautiful folds of flesh, *verbum caro factum est,* cannibalism the easy way minus priest and diploma, those sad bovine eyes peering inquisitively out over truck panels belong to me, the half-grown heifer fattened for the butcher and his gleaming knife is me, the flame that faithful wasps return to only to burn with the others in their flaming nest gives me a fairly good idea of the flaming honeycomb that awaits only me,

I am a corresponding member of the Academy of Palavery, a student in the Euphoria Department, my god is Dionysus, a sozzled, winsome lad, Good Cheer turned man, ironic Socrates is my Church Father, conversing patiently with one and all, hoping to lead them by his words or their tongues to the threshold of ignorance, Jaroslav Hašek is his first-born son and inventor of the beer-hall story, he had a gift for living and writing life, for humanizing the prosaic heavens, and his human qualities made the others feel uncomfortable with their pens,

I peer unflinchingly into the three blue dolls of this Holy Trinity without reaching the peak of emptiness, drunkenness without alcohol, education without knowledge, *inter urinas et faeces nascimur,* and our mothers sometimes seem to give birth to us straddling the crematory furnace or in the grass of unattended graves, I am a bull deblooded by laughter whose brain is being eaten with a spoon, like ice cream. Waiter, is there any more of that gulash?

—B.H.

P.S. As I analyze this text, which is meant as an introduction to a collection of my stories and which I wrote in five hours during irregular pauses between chopping wood and mowing grass, and which has the easygoing pulse of the vertical ax and the reed scythe's horizontal swish, I feel I must distinguish between the shoots that grew naturally out of my inner experience and the offshoots I acquired by reading. I must name the authors whose words have so fascinated me from the time I first read them that I regret not having come up with them myself. "I do not think of myself as a rosary, I think of myself as a broken chain of laughter" is an inverted variant of Nietzsche's "I am not a link in a chain, I am the chain itself." "Every love object is the center of a garden of paradise" is an exact quote from Novalis. *"Verbum caro factum est"* is St. John: "The word became flesh." "Dionysus . . . Good Cheer turned man" is Herder. *"Inter urinas et faeces nascimur"* is probably St. Augustine: "We are born between urine and feces." "Our mothers . . . give birth to us . . . in . . . open graves" is a Spanish schoolman whose name has slipped my mind. And that is all.

Contents

Introduction, Daniel S. Miritz   v

Author's Preface, "Handbook for the Apprentice
  Palaverer"   xiii

Romance   1

Palaverers   23

Angel Eyes   35

A Dull Afternoon   49

Evening Course   63

The Funeral   75

The Notary   81

At the Sign of the Greentree   103

Diamond Eye   113

A Prague Nativity   123

Contents

Little Eman   145

The Death of Mr. Baltisberger   157

The World Cafeteria   175

Want to See Golden Prague?   187

ROMANCE

I

Gaston Košilka had been standing for some time in front of the grocery store. When he looked into the show window at his face again, all he saw was a confirmation of what he had long known: that he did not like the way he looked, that he was an altogether uninteresting young man, the kind who was even more depressed when he came out of the movies than when he went in. Studying his face in the glass, he was certain that, with a build like his, he could never be what he dreamed of being. Fanfan the Tulip.

And just as he began torturing himself again over his reflection in the door, a gypsy girl opened it from the inside and came out onto the street carrying half a loaf of bread. Gaston was surprised by what the girl was wearing: two aprons—one in front and one in back—held together by safety pins. As she stood on the curb looking both ways before crossing, Gaston could not tell her back from her flat-chested front.

He wiped the sweat from his brow and said, "Well, what do you know about that!"

The gypsy girl turned around, her painted lips and the whites of her eyes shone out at him in the night, and she was about to say something when her voice failed her. Then she carried the hemisphere of the half-loaf of bread beside that black hair of hers and the white crust sketched her path in the darkness. She stopped in front of a lighted clothes store window, stuck out her hips, and looked over at Gaston out of the corner of her eye.

Gaston plucked up his courage and crossed the street too.

"How about a smoke?" she said. She made an upright V with her middle and index fingers.

Gaston placed a cigarette between her fingers and, lighting it for her, he said debonairly, "Your hair is so fragrant."

"Your hands are so shaky."

"I work hard," he said, blinking.

"What do you do?"

"Plumber's assistant," he said, blushing.

"Oh, a real man. Say, how much is that sweater over there?" she asked in a deep alto.

"Which one? That one?"

"No, the pink one."

"Forty-five crowns."

"Okay, I'll tell you what. You buy me the sweater, I take the bread back to my sister, and we'll go have a good time. You'll see," she promised, and when she took a drag, her cheeks collapsed and her eyes shone.

"What will I see?" he asked, a little frightened.

"You'll see. First buy me the sweater, and then you'll see. I swear to high heaven I'll be good to you," she said, raising her two fingers holding the cigarette in an oath.

"For that measly little sweater?"

"For that measly little sweater."

"But they're closed."

"That doesn't matter. Just hand over the jack, and I'll buy the sweater tomorrow."

"The jack?"

"Right, the jack," she said, spitting away the cigarette butt and rubbing her thumb against her index and middle finger.

"Oh! The jack!" said Gaston, finally catching on. "Cross my heart, I'll give it to you."

"The Virgin Mary will haunt you every night if you don't. I swear she will!" she threatened, and her face was grave yet absolutely unlined, and she looked him deep in the eyes with eyes like Lollobrigida's that seemed to fill up half her face. Then all of a sudden, as if she had just made a great discovery, she announced, "This is the way your eyes look," and made the letter O out of her thumb and index finger.

"Well, yours look like two wells."

"Like two wells," she said, completely unfazed. "When gypsy girls are young, everything about them is beautiful. And I am young." She made another upright V with her fingers.

Gaston tenderly placed a cigarette between them. Then he lit one up for himself too. He glanced over at the glass of the display window, pulled himself up a little, and took a brave look at the passing crowd. People were turning to look at him. Suddenly he wished that all his friends and relatives would just happen to walk down the street and see him standing up close to the pretty gypsy, gazing into her eyes and smoking. Now they were walking together. And even if her shoes were all raggedy, she took tiny little steps just like a lady.

"Great," he said, and gave a little skip.

"What's great?"

"Everything," he said, and squeezed her arm: a neighbor was coming down the street on her way home from shopping.

"Good evening, Mrs. Funděrová," said Gaston politely, just to make sure she had noticed him.

Mrs. Funděrová put down her package, looked him up and down and, seeing he was holding the girl by the arm, could hold back no longer. "Oh, your poor, poor mother."

The gypsy turned down a small street that led to the river. She was exhaling in deep sighs. The street was quiet and run down, the kind of street where anything might turn up, where anything might happen. A tall gas lamp stood in front of a dilapidated building resembling a Tyrolean farmhouse. A flight of wooden stairs led up to the second floor. One section of the rotten banister had fallen off and was hanging down like a ladder.

The floury-white crust of the bread shone in the dark, and when the gypsy tore off a hunk and began chewing it, it gleamed like the whites of her Arabian eyes.

"I walked down this street one day. It felt so strange," he confided to her. "It was pouring rain, and right here, in the light of this gas lamp, there were three gypsy brats singing and dancing, the water just streaming off them. They just kept on singing their 'gragra gloglo' and weaving in and out of their dance. It was raining cats and dogs, and all of a sudden those kids made me feel good inside."

"Those were my sister's kids," she said, putting her foot on the first step. "Want to come up with me?"

"Sure, but what about your sister?"

"Oh, she's gone hops-picking with the kids."

"Then who's the bread for?"

"My brother, but he's at work." She ran up the stairs and turned around at the top to give Gaston directions. "Look out, there's a board missing there. That's right. No, don't step on that one." Gaston grabbed for the banister but it crashed to the ground. When he had finally made his way up to the top he could see the stars through a hole in the roof. The gypsy was in good spirits, and as she frisked around he heard a crumbling under the wooden floor and the thud of something falling into the courtyard. She took him by the hand and kicked open a door that gave out a long groan. Then they went through a dark hallway, and when she opened another door and stepped into the room, Gaston's mouth dropped open in amazement.

"Well, what do you know about that!"

One of the two windows was lit by the gas lamp, which grew out of the sidewalk to shine in onto the floor of the large, empty room. Its light bounced off a mirror lying on the window sill, casting on the ceiling a silver rectangle that rained down a fine, gentle, misty kind of light, a light that brought into play all the tiny crystals in the Venetian chandelier, which hung glittering from the ceiling, glittering like a jewelry store. The ceiling arched into a vault like a white, four-pronged umbrella.

"That chandelier—where did you . . . uh . . . ?"

"What? The chandelier? Oh, you mean where did we swipe it from?" she asked, giving an imitation of a thief about to pounce on something.

"Well . . . yes . . . where did you swipe it from?"

"May all my children drop dead on the spot," she replied angrily, putting the bread on the other window sill, "if we didn't buy it at a junk shop. My sister, she could have bought a kitchen, but she wanted the chandelier," and so saying, she ran across the room, flitting past a large floor-to-ceiling mirror.

Gaston turned to follow her and caught a second glimpse of the Venetian chandelier, this time reflected in the mirror, but still radiating light like a candlelit Christmas tree.

"We're no run-of-the-mill gypsies, you know," she said, getting into first ballet position. "Our grandfather was a gypsy baron! He wore a jacket and carried a bamboo cane, and one of my sisters would open doors for him and another one would keep his shoes polished. So there!" But just as she stuck her nose in the air she began to cough.

"Okay, okay, but why do you have such a bad cold?"

"Gypsies always have colds. Once we went to the theater to see *Carmen*. Carmen was a gypsy, and she sang like she had a cold."

"Where do you work?"

"Me? Where I sleep. In the brick factory. I cook and keep the place clean." With a sigh she picked up a newspaper and went over to the window to read by the light of the gas lamp.

Gaston felt his face in the mirror. The Venetian chandelier grew out of his head; it sprayed out arches of glass diamonds like a gushing fountain. He could also see the gypsy girl in the mirror. She was sitting on the window sill reading her white newspaper. And when he thought about what his friends would think if they could see him here, when he pictured them going berserk and turning green with envy, he started whirling giddily around the room and let out a yelp of joy.

"Hey, you! Czech!" called the gypsy girl, jumping down from the window sill. "How about the forty crowns? You won't regret it. Gypsy girls are nice and clean." As proof she lifted the two pinned-together aprons and pointed to her shiny white panties in the mirror.

"Forty crowns, all right?" she said, pressing up against him.

He put his arms around her the way he had seen it done in the movies, but after caressing her protruding shoulder blades, he caught himself and said, "No, sir. Thirty-five crowns or nothing."

"All right then, thirty-five. But right away."

"No, not until afterward. Not until I see, as you put it."

"I know your kind. You're all the same. First you promise the world, then you kick a girl when she's down."

"Not me!" said Gaston, pulling himself up. "Listen, when I promise something, I do it."

"All right, okay. Just let me see the jack. You don't know how much I want that sweater." She took the hand he had held out to her and put it on her chest. "Just think how pretty it'd make me." She put both arms around him, clasping her hands together at the back of his neck. He reached for his wallet and picked out a bill, hoping against hope it would not be a hundred. It was a fifty.

"Man, are you loaded!" she cried, and stood up on her tiptoes and touched her forehead to his. Then, turning until the corners of their eyes were touching, she slowly moved her head back and forth. Their eyes seemed to be pressing to-gether. Then she blinked her eyelashes into his and said, "Well, let's get a move on. Or how about here?"

"No," he said, swallowing hard and removing a long black strand of hair from between his lips. "No. Mama's away, so we can go up to our place. We'll put on some coffee and some jazz, and . . ."

The gypsy girl finished his sentence with a series of bitter-almond kisses, and Gaston looked into the mirror with one eye, and the mirror was a movie screen. "What luxury," she said into his other eye. "Nobody at home, nobody, nobody. Nobody but the two of us and the coffee and jazz!"

He hugged her again, and—after checking himself out in the mirror—said, "You're terrific, Julinka."

"My name's not Julinka, and how about forking over the dough?"

"Okay. Here it is."

And he watched himself giving the girl the fifty-crown note in the mirror movie screen.

She took it, spat on it lightly, folded it three times, rolled up one of her aprons, and stuck it behind the elastic band of her white panties.

Under the influence of the whiteness of the bread, the news-paper, the panties, and the gas lamp, whose light was reflected by the mirror onto the ceiling, Gaston put his arms around the gypsy, kissed her, and then took her by the waist the way Gérard Philippe used to do in the movies. He noticed that the girl had put her hand over the bank note.

They went out into the hallway, where the stars were shining through the roof. Gaston laughed and said, "Well, what do you know about that!" and then added, "My aunt says that unless gypsies are fifteen to a room they feel like they've been abandoned. Right?"

II

The only light in the room came from the tubes in the back of the radio and the green eye that indicated it was turned on. The mournful strains of a jazz band spilled out of the depths of the speaker, only to be overpowered in the foreground by the hoarse, scratchy voice of Louis Armstrong. He was probably sitting with his trumpet in his lap, and he was croaking more than singing, as if after the tenth drink or so he had finally settled down to thinking out loud about the way things used to be.

"Hey, lover," called the gypsy from underneath the cold blankets. "How about a cigarette?"

"The cigarettes are on the chair. Matches too."

Louis Armstrong stopped singing and picked up the trumpet in those black fingers of his, wrapped it in his handkerchief like a bottle of champagne, and joined in the melody about the girl on Blueberry Hill, sounding for all the world as though someone had been poking around at his liver or fed him a meal of ground glass.

"And don't set fire to the bed!"

"I won't. And what if I do? Hey, that guy sings the way I talk."

"He's black like you are too. And flick the ashes behind the bed."

"Okay, lover. Hey, come over here."

"Should I turn on the lights?"

"No, people look better in the dark, but . . ."

"But what?" cried Gaston, jumping up. "You wouldn't even let me unpin your aprons. All I got for trying was a bloody finger. Why all these 'buts'?"

"I keep thinking you're going to kick me out."

"I ought to."

"Come over here, lover," she said, rolling over. "Let me sleep all night with you. When a gypsy girl sleeps with somebody, she falls in love."

"Don't set the bed on fire!"

She lifted the glowing cigarette as high as she could. "Don't worry. Hey, listen. I'm only thinking of you now. Please let me sleep here tonight. Please? You won't be sorry."

"But I have to get up early and go to work."

"So you think I'd rob you."

"That's not what I said, but . . ."

"A hell of a lot I'd get from you. And anyway, do you bastards think I don't know that our Ilonka used to come to this building? And that this is where she slit her wrists?"

"But I didn't have anything to do with it," he shouted, jumping up. Then, just as quickly sitting down again, he added, "It was our neighbor Franta. . . . Hey, what did you do with that cigarette?"

"What did you do with your eyes? I put it out in that box over there. But let me tell you. We'll catch up with your Franta someday. We'll get even. Don't you worry. We'll get even."

"Quit flopping all over the bed."

"Who do you think you're talking to anyway, Czech? I'm no beggar, you know. I have two changes of bed linen and curtains for two windows. And my grandfather was a baron and carried a bamboo cane and wore a blue jacket. You know, my curtains could really brighten up things here."

"Maybe. But why didn't you let me undo your aprons? Why? And why did I have to keep my hands around your neck? Tell me. Why?"

"You want to know why? 'Cause I was afraid you'd . . ." and she pantomimed a pickpocket plying his trade.

"You mean you thought I'd steal back the fifty crowns? You mean that's why you wouldn't let me undo your aprons?"

9

"We have to be very careful. . . . No, come sit beside me, baby. Listen. Supposing we started a new life together?"

"I've never tried that before."

"It's as easy as one, two, three. I'll teach you. First we pool everything we own, and if I do something you don't like, you can turn me out. But not till later. I can cook and keep house. I'd do your sewing and washing and bring you your dinner. And I'd let you take all my clothes off. Just as long as you don't run after other women."

"I don't even have a girlfriend."

"Good. That's the way it ought to be. I'd find out anyway and jump right into the Vltava. But supposing we went out dancing and somebody asked me for the next dance. What would you do?"

"What would I do . . ."

"You mean you'd let me dance with somebody else?" she cried, jumping out of bed.

"Wash your feet before you get into bed. Look how dirty they are," he said nervously.

"Glad to see you're a family man," she said, dusting off the soles of her feet. "But would you really let me go off and dance with somebody else?" When all he did was yawn and look at her with complete and utter lack of comprehension, she added, "You mean you wouldn't even slap me around a little?" and flopped down on top of the cool blankets. Gaston closed his eyes and began massaging his temples. He pictured his face early that evening in the grocery window and then later on in the mirror when the gypsy girl had been good to him, and then, here in bed, how frightened and then ashamed and awkward she had been. And after due consideration he said to her, "When I got finished with you, you wouldn't know what hit you!"

"There, I knew it. You *do* like me!" She bounced over onto her stomach and kicked her bare feet in the air.

"But I'm more the loner type," he said.

"Good. That's the way it ought to be," she said. "When we're home together, lover, you know what? I'll be there just like I wasn't there. Wait till you see how quiet a gypsy girl can be if her husband likes her that way."

"But before you know it, there'll be kids, and all the troubles they bring."

"What do you mean? I have a little girl myself. Her name is Margitka."

"Too bad. I always wanted blond kids."

"Your kids'll be blond, all right. Margitka is blond. Her father was a Czech. But when he started drinking on me, I threw him out. She's a pretty kid, too."

"Okay, okay, but where could she sleep?" he asked, scratching himself.

"Same place *I* slept. In a drawer or the wardrobe. She's getting on to three now. Soon she'll be going out to get you your cigarettes and beer, or hand you your slippers. How wide are your windows anyway?"

"Four feet."

She bounced over onto her back again.

"We're in luck," she exclaimed, euphoric. "Just right for my curtains. Will they give this place class! And just to show you I mean what I say"—she swung her legs off the bed and rolled up one of her aprons—"here's your fifty crowns back. We can use it for a nest egg, okay?" She took the folded bill out from under the elastic band of her panties and put it on the table in the glow of the radio's green eye.

"How old are you?" he asked.

"Eighteen. I'll be pretty for another ten years. How old are you?"

"Twenty-three."

"Couldn't be better. Fifteen good years ahead of you. But

just remember. If I went and danced with somebody else, you'd beat me black and blue."

"You bet I would!"

"Swear?"

"I swear."

"Good. Now I believe you. Wait till you see what a gypsy girl will do for the man she loves. Everyone will be jealous. You are my man. You are my lord and master. From now on you are my everything."

She spoke very solemnly, nodding to herself in agreement. And as she spoke, Gaston looked around the room. It looked dull and dreary. When he thought of the room with the Venetian chandelier and the gas lamp outside the window, he could not imagine anything he would rather do than pack up everything he owned, abandon his room forever, and move into the ghetto and that crumbling wreck of a building where you could see the stars through the ceiling in the hallway and read the evening papers by the light of the street lamp.

"But what will my mother say?" he asked.

"You leave that up to me. 'I count as a person too,' I'll tell her. And what if she says, 'You? Marry a gypsy? Over my dead body.' What will you say to that?"

"I'd say, 'Stretch out, Ma, I'm crossing over.'"

She puckered her lips. "This time for love."

His hands shook as he undid one safety pin and then the other and the two pinned-together aprons fell to the ground like a priestly robe.

And behind them three black voices sang a booming "My mama done told me," three black booming women standing on a ladder at the bottom of a well and dredging from the depths of their souls a song about the joys of those mournful "Blues in the Night."

III

A bird in the bushes lining the old mansion's façade gave the morning its first warbles and trills. Others joined it, until the morning air seemed saturated with them. Arm in arm with his gypsy girl, Gaston stopped in front of a glass case advertising the current attraction. What struck him most was a poster of Gérard Philippe holding a sword and wearing an open shirt.

"What I wouldn't give to be Fanfan the Tulip—just for a day," said Gaston longingly.

"Who? Him?"

"That's not just anybody, you know. That's Gérard Philippe. You know—Fanfan the Tulip."

"So what? Listen to me now, will you? You're a plumber's helper, and when somebody's toilet doesn't flush, who do they send for? You! When their water doesn't run, who do they call? You! They ought to make a movie about you and me, that's who they ought to make a movie about. Look, if you get a pay check every month and you help people into the bargain, what's the point of jumping from roof to roof with a sword in your hand? Wait till we get to the brick factory. Every second gypsy is a Fanfan—except they make bricks. And those bricks go into making buildings."

"But Gérard is so handsome."

"Him? Handsome?" she said, unpeeling a corner of the poster and tearing it down with a yank. "When we get married, I'll invite my cousins, the ones who shovel coal. Then you'll see four of your Gérards, one right after the other. I'll invite my grandfather too, the one with the blue jacket and the bamboo cane." She was very serious.

"You're every bit as handsome as my papa Demeter. He

used to carry me in his arms and smoke his cigarettes, and every once in a while he'd pass one back to Mama—she always walked behind him—so she could take a puff. He was a coal shoveler too, and people used to say he looked like an Indian chief."

On and on she talked, and as they walked along the Vltava, Gaston came to know for the first time in his life how a woman can build up a man's confidence. It was beginning to grow light. Here and there a fisherman sat bent over his bent-over rod. From an island in the middle of the river came the howling of a pack of German shepherds in pens and cages. The trees and bushes quivered with songbirds.

"To make it short and sweet, you're a plumber, and who's any better?"

"You know," said Gaston confidentially, "the guy I work with, the master plumber, he's impossible. He keeps insisting I call him by his first name. Now how can I call him by his first name when he's twenty years older than me? And when I told him I wouldn't feel right calling him by his first name, you know what he did? We were having a beer and he pointed his finger at me and shouted in front of all those people, 'I ask you, good people. Have you ever seen such a fool?'"

"Well, what do you know about that!" said the gypsy.

Gaston started laughing. "Sure, he was right to say, 'Look, if we're on a first-name basis, I'm your friend, and I can give you all kinds of tips on how to do things better and faster.' But all I could do was look him in the eyes and say, 'Don't be annoyed, sir, but you've got grown children. And when it comes to plumbing, I'm so far behind you it isn't funny.' And you know what he did? He pointed his finger at me again and shouted, 'Gaston here is trying to keep his distance from me. Have you ever seen such a fool?' And when he'd gone through that a few times, he lowered his voice and said, 'You've got to do me one better, Gaston. You've got to follow my every move so you can do it better. When a colt has sucked its mother dry, you know what it does, Gaston? It kicks her, that's what! Well, if that's what you want, it's war between us. No, not war. A concentration camp! We'll start carrying separate work kits too!' And he picked up our kit and threw my lunch out on the floor. And when I went to pick it up, he kicked it out of my hand."

"So your name is Gaston!" she said. "Gaston. Gaston. Well, let me tell you something, Gaston. Your name is nicer than Fanfan any day. But why *don't* you call him by his first name? You're his assistant, aren't you?" They had turned onto a bridge and paused while the gypsy girl stroked the rough surface of the railing.

"Feel it," she said to him. "You can still feel yesterday's sun on it. But why don't you call him by his first name?"

Gaston leaned over the railing, and then put his arms around the gypsy. "I'm shy."

He pointed down with his index finger.

There on the bank lay a huge naked gypsy under a comforter. He lay on his back, his upper torso exposed. He looked like a picture book, every inch of his body was covered with tattoos. The muscle of the arm behind his head was so big he used it for a pillow, and his mustache seemed like two horse tails. With his free hand the giant was smoking, looking up at the last star in the pale blue sky and smoking away. Beside him lay a curly head, its face buried in a pillow. The hitching pole of a wagon and backside of a horse, its tail whipping back and forth, stuck out from under the bridge's arch.

"Gypsies," said the gypsy girl proudly. "They must be from far away. Probably came to look for work, like we did last year."

"Why do they put the horse under the bridge and sleep outside in the dew themselves?"

"It takes time to get used to sleeping indoors. It took us time

15

too. When it's nice out, we all like sleeping outside. It's so stuffy when you're cooped up. . . . You know, my father Demeter was all tattooed, just like that guy down there. On Sunday we'd lie in bed with him and run our fingers over him like he was a picture book. And he would laugh and laugh. He was ticklish."

"How wonderful," said Gaston. "I didn't realize people like that still existed."

The curly head beside the tattooed giant turned over and brushed the willowy hair from its eyes. It was a gypsy woman, stretching and yawning. Then her man, his eyes still trained on the heavens, handed her his cigarette, and she too looked up at the morning sky and took a few puffs. Then she gave it back, and it was his turn to enjoy the blue smoke. People waiting for the tram had bent over the railing to watch them, but they kept on passing the cigarette back and forth and looking up into the now pinkish sky. The last star had just about gone out. Then the tram came.

They jumped onto the rear platform of the last car and remained standing. The gypsy girl was proud; she stood very erect and looked straight into the eyes of the people who had seen the two gypsies on the bank. But it was so early that most of them were either drowsing on their feet or staring down at the floor. The gypsy girl spotted a woman walking along the street and putting out gas lamps with a bamboo stick.

"My grandfather had a bamboo cane and a blue jacket," said the gypsy girl, "and when he met families on the street arguing and spitting at one another, all he had to do was pick up his cane and go like this"—and she drew a long dash in the air—"and that was the end of it. And if anybody dared to start up again, all he had to do was go like this with his finger"—and she made a beckoning signal—"and the gypsy had to go up to Grandfather and let himself be hit over the head with his cane. And no funny business."

"That sounds pretty unbelievable," said Gaston.

"May all our children drop dead on the spot if I'm lying!" And she licked her finger and raised it in an oath. "You know, being a baron, Grandfather also got to referee soccer. There they were: twenty gypsies on one side, twenty on the other, and Grandfather . . ."

"But in soccer there are only eleven men to a side," said Gaston, and no sooner had the words left his mouth than to his great consternation he caught sight of the master plumber he worked with. The next thing he knew, the plumber had gotten up out of his seat and was staggering over to them, looking first at Gaston and then at the gypsy girl, who was stamping her foot and saying, "Twenty on one side, twenty on the other. I should know. I was there. Grandfather refereed with his bamboo cane. He had a silver whistle on a yellow cord around his neck, and every time somebody kicked somebody else too hard, he would blow it real hard and go like this with his finger"—and she beckoned again—"and the one who had been caught roughnecking ran up, and Grandfather smacked him one over the head with his bamboo cane, because he was a gypsy baron. The one who was at fault would hold his head for a while and holler, and when it stopped hurting he'd go back into the game."

"That's the way *we* ought to play. And work. Eh, Gaston?" said the master plumber.

"Look, mister, you're drunk. Mind your own business, will you?" replied the gypsy with flashing eyes.

"This is my boss," said Gaston by way of introduction.

"You?" asked the gypsy.

"And this is my . . . fiancée," said Gaston.

"Gaston," said the plumber, shaking his head, "from now

on we share our work kit again. Last name, first name—call me whatever you please. You're the master now. You've proven yourself. I never had a gypsy girl myself. But oh, how I've dreamed about it." And he launched into a drunken version of a popular gypsy song.

The plumber put one foot on the outside step. A morning breeze ruffled his thinning hair. The tram was slowing down.

"Have you ever seen such a fool?" he said, pointing to himself, and with a bow he jumped off.

"Hey, Pavel! You been out drinking again?" called Gaston after him, leaning out of the tram. "Want me to see you home?"

The plumber waved back a sign of defeat that was clearly meant to acknowledge the superiority of youth. . . . On the hill where they got off, Gaston took the gypsy girl by the arm. "He's a good man, even if he does drink. He's all alone in the world. He was married and had kids, but when they got older his wife came and told him they weren't his and that she was leaving him for their real father, and thanks for bringing them up. . . . Whenever he gets to thinking about it, he'll tap his forehead and rub his eyes, take a drink from his stein, tell me the whole story again, and ask, 'Have you ever heard of such a thing, Gaston? And I'm the one it had to happen to.'"

Crossing a gully, they left the city limits and began walking along the brick-factory fence. Before long they came upon an old man standing under a locust tree with a shotgun in his hand.

"Who's there?" he asked.

"It's me, Pop," said the gypsy girl hoarsely.

"Aha! A band of thieves! Better watch out. No ifs, ands, buts, or three chances to turn back with me. I aim straight for the kisser!" yelled the old watchman, scared half to death.

"Hey, Pop, I'm just bringing one of your gypsy girls home!" yelled Gaston.

The old man went up to the gate and flung the shotgun back on his shoulder. "Why, you little monkey, you. You should have been in bed long ago," he said. "And who's that?"

"My sweetheart."

"Sweetheart! Bet he doesn't even know what your name is."

"You're right. I don't," said Gaston.

"But you knew enough to sleep with her. Just like in the good old days," he mused opening the gate. "You know," he said putting his arm around Gaston's shoulder, "you couldn't have done better. Just make sure you don't stop loving her. Once when I was walking through the woods I met a girl, and before we got to the first village I offered her my hand and she accepted. It wasn't until afterward we introduced ourselves. For two years we lived together in sin, but finally we did get married. . . . Did you just hear something?" He suddenly grew stiff and lifted one leg into the air like a pointer.

"No," whispered Gaston.

"That's good, because I hear more than I see. So I keep having this dream about being mugged by thieves after the cashbox."

As they walked along through the pink fog and blue grass, Gaston said, "It's a tough job you've got here."

"I'll say," the watchman sighed, "but I enjoy it. So you've got yourself a gypsy. Brave man, brave man. You can't go wrong, as long as you keep a firm hand on the reins. . . . If you do, your life together will be heaven. My wife came from the wagons too. And did she ever wander! . . . But you, you little tramp, you look cold. Come on, young man, let me show you where your Margit sleeps."

"Margit. What a pretty name!"

The gypsy girl smiled through her shivers and sniffles. Then the old watchman pointed to a tiny grove of locust trees spotted with comforters sheltering sleeping gypsies, some all sprawled out, others wound up into little balls, and still others looking for all the world as if they had been shot the night before. But all of them were breathing regularly in deep, healthy sleep. Here and there the brickmakers' accommodations were decorated by a child's locks and ringlets.

"They've got their own little houses over there, but as soon as summer and the hot nights come along, they all move out here. Too stuffy for them inside. It's that hot blood, you know," snickered the watchman.

Down below, Prague had begun to emerge from the blue haze. The electric lights were still on. Strung like garlands from street to street, they gave the city the appearance of a circus someone had forgotten to close down. The tower on Petřín Hill still had its red warning lights on, and a ruby glowed on the lightning rod that topped the tall chimney on Střešovice Hospital. But up here a pack of tired gypsies sprinkled with dead locust blossoms slept on into the morning— gypsies, onetime nomads who not so long ago, in earrings and hunting caps, rode their wagons into Prague to exchange their romantic roving ways for a life of everyday work.

"I can't sleep under a tree," said the gypsy through her coughing. "When blossoms fall on my face, I dream that there's moths sitting on my head, or it's snowing." She was trying to keep warm by jumping from one foot to the other. "'By, Gaston. See you tomorrow. I'll wait for you in front of the Fanfan pictures. Or why don't you go straight to our house? You know where. See you!" She jumped over one of the sleepers and turned around at an elderbush to wave again. Then the two pinned-together aprons collapsed, and she slipped under a comforter with a pair of children.

"Let's get going," said the old watchman, dragging himself off on his rounds again. "The thieves here are so fierce that if they can't get in any other way they're liable to come down through the ceiling. Well, they better watch their step when

I'm around. 'Cause nobody gets a second chance with me. I just go ahead and shoot, that's all. So you've got yourself a gypsy girl, eh?" But Gaston was watching a little gypsy boy who had wriggled out from under the comforter and waddled over to the edge of the grove to pee a great arc over all of the city lying at his feet.

"Who can tell?" said the watchman. "That little tyke might just be president someday. . . . So you've got yourself a gypsy girl. But what will they say at home? Supposing your mama says, 'A gypsy? Over my dead body.' What will you say then, huh?"

"I'll say, 'Stretch out, Ma, I'm crossing over. That gypsy girl has put me back on my feet.'" And with one hand on his hip he looked down into the valley. A streetcar that looked like a harmonica was crossing a white bridge. The morning sun glittered in its windows.

PALAVERERS

I

Some old men sitting on a bench in front of the cement factory were shouting at one another, grabbing one another by the lapels, and hollering into one another's ears.

It was drizzling cement dust, and all the houses and gardens were coated with finely ground limestone.

I walked out into the dusty field.

A little man with a sickle was mowing grass under a lone pear tree.

"Excuse me, but who are those old men over by the gate-keeper, the ones who are yelling and screaming at each other?"

"At the main gate? Those are our pensioners," said the little man without interrupting his mowing.

"Nice way to grow old," I said.

"Isn't it though?" said the man. "I can't wait to join them. Only a few years now."

"Hope you make it!"

"Oh, don't worry about me. This part of the country is good for the health. Average age here is seventy," said the man, and continued his skillful one-handed mowing. Cement dust poured out of the grass like smoke from a fire that has just been doused with water.

"But can you tell me what the old men are arguing about? What makes them scream at each other all the time?"

"They like to watch the cement factory at work. They think they could do better. Anyway, the more they shout, the thirstier they are at night. They worked there all their lives, you know. They grew up with that factory. They couldn't live without it."

"But why don't they go pick mushrooms? Or why don't they just pack up and settle somewhere near the border? They'd each get a little house and a plot of land out in the woods." I wiped my nose with the back of my hand. It left a slimy black line.

"Well, let me tell you," said the man, and stopped his mowing. "One of the old timers by the name of Mareček moved out to the woods the other side of Klatovy. Two weeks later he came back in an ambulance. The fresh air gave him asthma. Two days later he was his old self again. That one over by the gate, the one that's yelling the loudest—that's Mareček. Believe you me, our air here is as tough as a solid pair of haunches, as thick as pea soup."

"I don't like pea soup," I said, stepping under the pear tree.

A team of horses galloping past us on the dusty road kicked up a cement screen so thick that it completely blocked out the cart they were drawing. The driver just kept singing his cheerful song inside the cloud of dust. Suddenly the gelding on the right gave a jerk on the reins, tore some of the smaller branches off the pear tree, and shook down a good hundred pounds of cement dust. I groped my way out of the cloud, my arms stretched in front of me.

I soon noticed that, though I'd started out in a dark suit, I was now wearing a gray one.

"Can you please tell me where Jirka Burgán lives?" I asked.

The man was back at his mowing, balancing his weight as

before with his free hand. Just then his sickle hit a molehill and, with a sudden leap, he darted out into the fields.

"Wasps!" he yelled. And he brandished the sickle above his head.

I ran to catch up with him. "Excuse me, but can you tell me where Jirka Burgán lives?"

"I'm Jirka's father," he called back, still on the run, lashing out at the aggressive wasps with his sharp sickle.

"Pleased to meet you. I'm a friend of Jirka's," I said by way of introduction.

"He'll be happy to know you're here. He's been expecting you," yelled Mr. Burgán, and put on a burst of speed.

But in the midst of waving his sickle around and lashing out at the wasps, what did he do but drive the sickle into his own unlucky skull. He didn't stop running, though, and was always slightly ahead of me, the sickle sticking out of his skull like a feather in a cap.

We stopped at the gate to his house. Not even his nostrils showed the sign of a tremor. Blood streamed down his dust-laden hair and around both ears, coming together in fast-falling drops below his chin.

"Let me pull it out for you," I said.

"There's no rush. Our boy may want to do a picture of me like this. Here comes my wife."

A heavy-set woman had come through the gate, her sleeves rolled up and her hands greasy. She might have just finished gutting a goose. One of her eyelids hung lower than the other, and her lower lip sagged.

"I've been keeping an eye out for you," she said, kneading my hand. "Welcome, welcome."

Then rosy-cheeked Jirka came running through the gate. He shook my hand with one hand and motioned toward the countryside with the other. "Beautiful, isn't it? Have I been lying or haven't I? What colors! What a landscape! What fresh air!"

"Lovely, lovely, but look what's happened to your father," I said.

"What's wrong?" asked Jirka, looking around.

"What's wrong? Why, this!" I answered, wiggling the sickle that stuck out of Mr. Burgán's head like a gigantic beak.

"Ouch," said Mr. Burgán.

"Oh, that," said my friend with a wave of the hand. "I thought something really bad had happened. Look, Mother! Father must have been after those wasps again. Naughty, naughty!" Turning to me, he laughed and said, "We always have such fun. Once when someone had been stealing our rabbits, Father decided to teach them a lesson, so he laid down some boards over the manure pit in such a way that if anyone even set foot on them at night they'd fall straight in. You see, the rabbit hutch is right next to the pit. Well, wouldn't you know: Father forgot all about it and fell in the next morning himself."

"It's not all that deep," said Mr. Burgán.

"How deep is it?" asked Jirka, leaning over toward his father for the answer.

"Oh, up to here," said Mr. Burgán, holding his hand up to his throat.

"There, you see!" roared Jirka. "Then there was the time he decided to play sanitary engineer. He poured a bucket of carbide into the outhouse and emptied his pipe into it a few minutes later. I happened to be leaving the house at the time, and what should I see? An explosion like a cannon shot, a quarter of a ton of flying feces, and Father, twenty feet off the ground, somersaulting his way through the middle of it all! He was lucky though: the manure broke his fall."

"Ho ho ho ho ho." Mrs. Burgánová laughed so hard her belly shook.

"That's not true. I wasn't any twenty feet above that manure," said Mr. Burgán, beaming. The blood around his ears was beginning to dry into an enamel gleam.

"How high was it then?" asked Jirka, leaning over again for the answer.

"Oh, around fifteen, say. And there couldn't have been more than a fifth of a ton of fecal matter," answered Mr. Burgán. "Our son is always exaggerating," he added. "It's the artist in him."

"That'll do it every time," I said. "Now please don't get me wrong, Mr. Burgán, but that sickle in your head is making me nervous."

"Oh, it's nothing," said Mrs. Burgánová and, taking hold of the handle, she wiggled it a few times to loosen it and then yanked it out of the wound.

"Couldn't Mr. Burgán get blood poisoning?" I asked, concerned.

"No. We treat everything here with fresh air," answered Mrs. Burgánová and, lovingly making a fist, she punched her husband in the forehead. "It's always a good idea to give Father a punch between the horns first thing in the morning. Why? Because he's a naughty boy." She took her husband by the hair and dragged him into the yard and, shoving his blood-stained head under the pump with one hand, she began to pump with the other.

"Father certainly has a lot of energy in him," said Jirka. "This year during his vacation he spent some time fixing the drainpipe. He would walk all around the edge of the roof laughing, and never thought to strap himself down to anything. Mother stood watch on the cement walk so if he fell she could run for the ambulance. On the fourteenth day Father finally strapped himself down, and fell off the roof. There he was, hanging by one leg. I passed him things to drink through the window while Mother spread out all our quilts on the cement walk.

And what do you think happened when I cut him down? He fell headfirst right alongside the quilts on the cement."

"Ho ho ho ho." That was Mrs. Burgánová again. "Right onto the cement. But by nightfall he was down at the tavern again," she added, pumping away.

"Father rides a motorcycle, too," said Jirka in a loud voice so that his father could hear. "Our friends who drive tell us, 'No offense meant, but the way your father follows the safety rules you'll be bringing him home in a basket one of these days!' Ha ha ha! One day when Father didn't come home we took a basket and went out looking for him. Well, down the road a ways, we came to a curve with some thornbushes, and all of a sudden we hear a sort of bleating coming from them. We go over to investigate, and what did we see, Mother?"

"Ho ho ho ho." Mrs. Burgánová was still holding her husband's head under the pump.

"There was Father and his motorcycle wedged into a thornbush!" said Jirka, almost choking with laughter. "Instead of taking the curve, he'd driven straight into the bushes. So anyway there he was, sitting on the motorcycle with his hands on the handlebars, unable to move for two whole hours. The thorns and nettle and thistle branches had held him in place."

"I had one thorn up my nose and one under my eyelid, and was I dying for a sneeze!" Mr. Burgán yelled over, raising his head. But Mrs. Burgánová grabbed him by the hair and shoved his head back down under the pump.

"And how did you get him out?" I asked with a shudder.

"First I brought over the sheepshears, then the garden shears. I performed what we call a Preisler incision and had him out of there within the hour," said Jirka.

Mr. Burgán raised his head to add something but slammed the back of his neck against the pump's iron spout in the process.

Suddenly there was a flash of lightning over a nearby hill and the sound of an explosion from the same direction.

"Ten o'clock," said Jirka.

"The rascals," his mother said tenderly and looked up at the hill, where a small white cloud was forming just above a clearing. A number of soldiers appeared from among the dust-laden pine trees up on the hill, and now one of them came out into the clearing and on a flag signal released the safety on his hand grenade, hurled it into another clearing, and dove for cover. There was another explosion and another milky cloud. The force of the blast reached all the way down into the valley, shaking cement dust from hazel shrubs and sunflowers.

"The rascals," said Mrs. Burgánová gently. She pulled her husband away from the pump by his hair, then parted the hair near the wound, and examined it with great concern. "It'll dry up just fine in the fresh air," she said, and politely motioned to me to come into the house.

II

The kitchen was hung with dozens of dust-laden pictures. Moving a chair around from picture to picture, Mrs. Burgánová huffed and puffed her way up to each canvas and dusted it off with a wet rag. Bright, dazzling colors suddenly lit up the room.

Every five minutes explosions from the army training camp would shake the house and rattle all the cups and saucers in the buffet. With every hand grenade, the brass bed would roll a little farther out of place on its casters. Each time, Mrs. Burgánová would look in the direction of the explosion, and each time she would say tenderly, "The rascals . . ."

Meanwhile Mr. Burgán, using his sickle for a pointer, had begun to show me the pictures.

"Now when our son painted this 'Sunset over a Pond in Southern Bohemia' he wore shoes that were one size too small for him. And when he did this 'Karlstein Scene' he hammered a quarter-inch nail into his own heel through the heel of his shoe. And while he was working on this 'Birch Forest outside Litomyšl' he didn't do number one all day. And when painting 'Horses at Pasture near Přibyslav' here, he stood up to his waist in a smelly bog. And before setting to work on 'From a Mountain Peak,' he fasted for three days."

While Mr. Burgán talked, Mrs. Burgánová moved her chair around to each picture, huffing and puffing her way up to the canvas and wiping it off with a wet rag. Every five minutes she would look through the wall in the direction of the explosion and say tenderly, "The rascals."

By the time the church bell rang noon, the brass bed had rolled clear across the room.

Mr. Burgán pointed to the last picture and said, "Our son calls this one 'Winter Mood,' and before he painted it he took off his shoes, rolled up his pants, and stood observing the scene in a freezing cold stream in the middle of January."

"The rascals," said Mrs. Burgánová, and climbed down from the chair.

For a while the silence was oppressive.

Mrs. Burgánová pushed the brass bed back across the kitchen.

"The pictures are beautiful. They show deep feeling," I said. "But why did Jirka have to wear shoes a size too small for him? Why did he have to hammer a nail into his heel? Why did he have to stand barefoot in that freezing water? Why?"

Jirka's eyes were glued to the floor. His face was burning with embarrassment.

"You see," said Mr. Burgán, "our boy doesn't have any formal training, so he makes up for it with experiences he feels deeply. And, well, that's why we asked you out here. We were wondering whether our son could go to Prague to study art."

"Jirka, you paint your landscapes from nature, don't you?" I asked. "Where do you go for those superb colors? The way you juxtapose blue and red. Why, the Impressionists would be proud of your colors. Where do you find them?"

Mr. Burgán drew back the curtain with his sickle. A fine powder issued from the material.

"See that?" asked Mr. Burgán. "See those colors out there? Nearly all the pictures hanging in the kitchen were painted in this part of the country. Just look at that riot of color."

Mr. Burgán held the curtain back so I could share his view of a countryside as gray as a herd of old elephants. As soon as anything moved, up rose long streamers of cement dust. A tractor pulling a reaper through a gray alfalfa field stirred up the sort of gray cloud that follows a cart on a dusty road. Two or three fields farther on, a young farm hand was loading sheaves of rye, and each time he picked up a sheaf the dust and fumes it gave off were so dense he seemed to be setting it on fire.

"Just look at those colors," said Mr. Burgán, the sickle trembling in his hand.

Up in the clearing, an infantryman released the safety of his grenade and threw it with all his might. The brass bed started across the kitchen again. For the first time Mrs. Burgánová made no response.

"The rascals," I said.

She put her hand on my sleeve—one of her eyelids hung down like a pancake—and said to me in a motherly tone, "Not you. You—never. We're the only ones allowed to call them names. We're not calling them names anyway; we're only blowing off steam. It's a game we play. They're our soldiers, after all. It's the same in your family now, isn't it?

31

Within the family circle you can do whatever you please. You can call your family names, you can tell them where to go. But only within the family circle. It doesn't work with outsiders. Jirka and me, we're the only ones who can make fun of Father . . . no one else. . . . But what's your opinion? Should our boy go to Prague? Will he do anything there for Czech art?"

She looked at me with knowing eyes, eyes with the power of penetrating the depths of my soul.

"Prague is like a pair of obstetric forceps," I said, looking down, "and these pictures, they're no child's play. They're the finished product. As far as I can tell, he's got a good chance of making a name for himself."

"We'll see," said Mrs. Burgánová.

Mr. Burgán opened the door and beckoned to me with the sickle.

"Our boy is a sculptor too. Look at this," he said, tapping his sickle on a magnificent plaster statue. "This is 'Bivoj without His Boar.'"

"Why, that's amazing! What biceps!" I said. "Jirka, who was your model? Was he a weight lifter, a heavyweight?"

Jirka was again staring down with embarrassment.

"Neither weight lifter nor heavyweight. . . . Me!" said Mr. Burgán, pointing to himself with the sickle.

"You?"

"Me," repeated Mr. Burgán gleefully. "What an imagination our boy has. When he hears the faucet dripping, he picks up his pencil and draws Niagara Falls. When he scratches his finger, the first thing he does is find out how much a third-class funeral costs. Minimum cause, maximum effect," added Mr. Burgán with a wink.

"I can't get over how well you understand these things, Mr. Burgán," I said.

"Oh, that's because I'm from Vršovice," he said, scratching his head with the sickle. "Have you ever seen Shakespeare's *Troilus and Cressida?* Just about a quarter of a century ago I had a walk-on part in it at the Vinohrady Theater. In the fifth act the director needed two beautiful naked statues to decorate the palace. One of them was played by me, painted bronze, the other by a girl, painted bronze. During the fifth act of every performance we would lie motionless in the glare of the spotlights with the stagehands looking down at us—mostly at the pretty girl though. Then, when *Troilus and Cressida* was over, I asked that naked statue to marry me and she said yes, and the result is we've been living together for a quarter of a century."

"Is that your bronze statue?" I asked.

Mr. Burgán nodded and smiled.

"The one that lay there with you during the fifth act?" I asked.

Mr. Burgán nodded and smiled.

"Why don't we let in some fresh air?" suggested Mrs. Burgánová.

Some cement dust drizzled in onto the rug.

"If you ever feel your nerves need a rest," said Mrs. Burgánová, "you ought to think about coming and spending, say, a whole week with us."

"What about the grenades? Are they always like that?" I asked.

"Oh no," said Mrs. Burgánová, taking a vacuum cleaner out of a cabinet. "Only Monday through Saturday from ten to three. Sunday is so sad. The silence is so perfect it makes an awful racket. So we listen to the radio and Jirka plays his helicon all day. We can hardly wait to go to sleep, because we know that when we wake up it won't be long before we have our soldiers back."

33

"Did you really both lie naked and bronzed on that stage? Really?"

"Really," said Mrs. Burgánová, waddling over to her husband and handing him a rolled-up cord with a plug at the end. "Father, go and vacuum off the aster bush near the wall. I want to make Jirka's friend a bouquet. The rascals . . ." she added tenderly, and looked out the window to the hill, where a small white cloud had formed just above the clearing. It was like a white hawthorn bush in bloom.

ANGEL EYES

"Where's the boss?" he asked the young salesgirl.

She pointed to the door and said, "The boss's wife is in the garden, and the boss is probably out back in the bakery. And who are you?"

"I represent the insurance company," he answered.

Some customers came into the store, and the girl asked them whether she could help them. The customers bought some rolls and bread, and soon a new group of customers came in. The salesgirl pointed to the door again. "The boss's wife is in the garden; the boss is out back in the bakery."

The insurance agent went into the hall, where row upon row of sweet-smelling loaves of bread were set out on racks, and stopping at the window he looked out into the garden, where a woman was walking barefoot under the apple trees. She had just bent over, and from a pile of dewy apples she chose the most beautiful and put it into the pocket of her apron. Then she picked up another, cleaned and polished it against her apron, took a long look at it, and then bit into its sweep pulp. The sound of her sinking her teeth into the apple and then crunching it with obvious relish reached as far as the hallway. Then, lost in thought, she waded through the fallen leaves and damp grass until she came to a weeping willow; she pushed aside the dangling branches and stood watching an old man in a wheel chair. The old man, all bundled up in a blanket, was

35

reading a large book attached to a music stand. He looked like a bird in flight. The woman walked up to the stand, turned the page, and fastened it with a clothespin to keep the wind from blowing it around. She patted the old man on the head and straightened his blanket for him, while he, with a simple-minded smile, read on. Once again she pushed aside the branches and started off through the wet grass. By the time she appeared at the window her feet were bright red.

She walked into the corridor and stopped before the insurance salesman in a provocative stance. She squinted at a second apple and bit into it, again with great relish, making an audible wound in the sweet pulp. Finally she looked up quizzically.

The insurance salesman introduced himself and said that the master baker, Mr. Beránek, had originally signed an application to join the Small Businessmen's Association but then had sent in a letter saying that he wished to cancel his membership and have his money returned. What did she, Mrs. Beránek, have to say about the matter? he wanted to know.

She threw away the stem of the apple, took a paper bag from the rack, set it down on the window sill, took out a pencil, and wrote a few figures on the bag, did some multiplying, and added up the results. "My husband is crazy. *He* may not be around when he's ninety, but *I* certainly will—just like my father," and she pointed to the old man in the wheel chair. "Even if I only live to be seventy-five, I'll make fifty thousand on that insurance." She picked up the pencil and underlined the sum she had come up with on the paper bag. Then she pointed to the door and shrugged her shoulders. "But he doesn't want to. He's always got some bee in his bonnet. When he was young, he would wake me up and scream, 'Out with it. Who did you sleep with before me?' and put me through the wringer. He still wakes me up all right, but now he waves that application blank in my face and roars, 'When that angel-eyed insurance agent comes back, here's what he'll find waiting for

him!' And he rams his fist into the bedboard until his knuckles
are drenched in blood. . . . That's just the way he is." She
crumpled up the paper bag with the figures on it, took out an
apple, polished it against her mighty bosom, and with great
relish bit into the pulp.

"What is your father reading?" he asked.

"The funny papers," she said with apple foam shining on
her teeth. "What else is there to do when you're paralyzed like
he is? He used to go around hawking those automatic needle
threaders. Do you know the kind I mean? Have you ever
seen one? No? Really?" She looked at him astounded. "You
can't mean that." And in pure, native huckster she began
reciting, "Mother comes trudging home from the fields. She
picks up her needle and thread but her eyes are weak, her
hands tremble. Try as she might, she just can't seem to get
the thread through that tiny hole. That's where my automatic
needle threader comes in. Ladies and gentlemen! I have sold
this world-renowned invention in Paris for five crowns, but
today I want everyone to be a winner, today I am letting it go
for a mere two crowns. And at no extra cost I will throw in one
large spool of white thread and one small spool of black along
with twelve—that's right, one whole dozen—needles. Let's everyone be a winner."

The whole time she was delivering her pitch, she looked the
insurance salesman straight in the eyes. He was close enough
to smell the fragrance of her breath, the moist, sweet fragrance
of the apple foam. He had the feeling she was giving him the
same kind of look she had given the apples she had just been
crunching. "You mean you never heard that?" she asked.

"Never," he said, letting out his breath and smiling. "Say,
aren't your feet getting cold? Walking around barefoot like
that on the tiles."

"No, I'm always hot, red hot."

And so saying, she leaned over close to the insurance salesman's lips. He could see her big beautiful eyes brimming with healthy sensuality, and the next thing he knew she had given him a long kiss. Her lips were cold and fragrant from the apples.

Suddenly she jumped away, frightened by the sound of an opening door. Her bare feet slapped the tiles. She stopped to listen, then smiled and said, "What beautiful eyes you have." And picking up a large wicker basket, she began filling it with loaves of bread. "If you ever want me the way I want you, you know where to find me." She lifted the heavy basket without the slightest effort and pointed her chin toward the door at the end of the hallway. "That's where *he* sleeps," she said, giving the insurance salesman a last glance at her beautiful eyes. Then she pushed open the shop door with her backside and swirled her way into the shop.

He stood for a while, listening, then looked over at the old man reading the funny papers under the willow tree. Finally he crossed the hallway and opened the door to the baker's workshop.

It was quiet. Loaf after loaf lined the racks along the walls, and stretched out on a cot beneath them lay Mr. Beránek in his long underwear. Lying on his stomach with one arm draped over the pillow, he looked as if he were trying to swim across the room. A slipper splattered with dried dough lay on the floor. The insurance salesman bent down and shook the sleeping figure, who responded by sitting up, yawning, and stretching until his bones cracked.

"Are you Mr. Beránek, the baker?" he asked.

But the baker had fallen back down on the bed and was already fast asleep.

The insurance man shook him again and asked, "Are you the one who wrote us the letter starting, 'Dear Dirty Bastards'?"

This time the baker jumped up, gave himself a shake, turned the insurance salesman around to the light, took his head between his monstrously large hands, looked him in the eyes as if he were about to smother him with kisses, and roared, "He's not the one! Where is that swine with the angel eyes?"

"What?" asked the startled insurance salesman, running his finger around his collar.

"Oh, my God!" cried out Mr. Beránek, hopping around the room in his long underwear. "To think that a man like me, who gives every insurance man who walks through my door a swift kick, as a matter of principle, to think that I signed up for that disgusting swindle! And I paid for it with the money I was going to invest in beechwood." To make his point, he gave himself such a punch in the forehead that his eyes started flickering. "If it hadn't been for those baby blue eyes of his! And you know what that son of a bitch asked me? Whether I'd rather have a house in the country or a house in the city as my premium when I go on pension. And whether I'd prefer to take my month-long all-expenses-paid vacation by the sea or in the mountains. And, jerk that I am, I told him to put me down for the country house and the mountains!" Which was followed by another self-inflicted punch in the forehead, so powerful this time that he fell back onto the cot. "I walked around on cloud nine until evening, opening the door of my new cottage, looking through binoculars at the mountains . . . That night I read the fine print, and when I finally waded through it I collapsed right here." He pointed to the cot. Then he sprang up, grabbed the insurance man by the sleeve, and dragged him over to the wall, where he tapped his cracked nails against some sums scribbled on the plaster. "You people cheated me!" he roared, underlining the sum with his finger. "I ought to cram this down your throat! For fifty thousand I would have had to pay back premiums to before I was born! And for what! That angel-eyed swine who wrote up the policy never even told me!" And his hands twisted into a cramp.

Suddenly his eyes began darting about the room. "Do you

know what I'm going to do to that guy if he and his blue eyes ever come back?" But nothing—not the rolling pin, the logs, or the fire hooks—seemed to inspire him. Not until his glance fell on the baker's shovels did he seem satisfied.

He grabbed one off the wall, ran the length of the room, raised it into a horizontal position, poised it carefully, took a running leap toward the oven wall, and rammed the shovel into it with all his might. The impact of the blow threw him down on his back, but he was triumphant. "That's how I'll cram it down his throat . . . and this is how I'll twist it around." And he gave a demonstration of how he would demolish the angel-eyed insurance agent. Picking himself up, the baker stayed on all fours long enough to complete the image. "They may cart *me* off to jail, but they'll take *him* straight to the morgue." Then he straightened up and sat down on the cot with his head in his hands.

The agent of the Small Businessmen's Association wiped the sweat from his brow. "Well, that's the living end!" he exclaimed, scandalized. "That's why the Association sent me to you, you know. Show me your application form, Mr. Beránek. I want to see who it was that signed you up."

The baker picked up his pillow, took out a case crammed full of all kinds of documents, found the application, and handed it to the insurance agent.

The agent unfolded the paper. "Aha! Now I understand! It was Krahulík! Mr. Beránek, give me your hand. Come on . . . that's right. Now, as a civil servant, I'm willing to bet you anything you like that our Mr. Krahulík will not only get the sack but will have to face the public prosecutor as well. How could he have done such a thing?" The agent was shocked. Then he added, "I'll bet Mr. Krahulík never even told you about the bonuses the state pays on all small businessmen's pensions. He didn't tell you about county or district bonuses either, did he?"

"Well, no, he didn't . . ." mumbled the baker.

"There, you see?" he said, and shook Mr. Beránek's hand. "Then he certainly never told you that our good President Beneš cares so much for his small businessmen that he himself saw to it that a definite percentage of the yields from the newly nationalized industries should be set aside for your pension. Which means that—let's see now, this is 1947—in ten years your pension will double. . . . How could he have failed to tell you that?"

"But he never said a word about it," croaked the baker.

"Then there's your problem in a nutshell! Cross my heart. That's what the insurance revolution is all about! What else did the millions give their lives for? Today's youth is going to pay for the older generation of small businessmen. Mr. Beránek, I'll see to it at the Ministry of Social Security that the whole affair is set aside, to give you time to think things over, and for the time being you won't pay a thing. It's as easy as that." And he took a stamp and stamp pad out of his brief case, breathed on the stamp, and pressed it painstakingly on the stamp pad. In the space next to "Dear Dirty Bastards" he stamped *My complaint has been taken care of.*

He handed the baker a pencil and authoritatively showed him where to sign.

Then he carefully folded up the letter and announced, "You can expect further information from our central office. You know, Mr. Beránek, once we cross you off our roster, that's the end. Even if you came to us on your knees we wouldn't take you back. Not that we wouldn't like to. It just doesn't work that way. The only way you can rejoin is by special dispensation from the minister." And leaning over one of the baskets, he summed up with "My, what appetizing rolls!"

"Open up your brief case," said the baker, and dumped in as many rolls as it would hold.

When they said good-by they stared into each others' eyes for a long moment.

In the hallway the insurance man gave a deep sigh, laid his brief case on the window sill, and leaned on it with both hands.

He looked out into the garden at the apples, still wet with dewdrops and now lying on a bed of straw. The baker's wife ran through the wet grass and without pausing pushed apart the willow branches. She turned over the next page of the funny papers and fastened it to the others with the clothespin to keep the wind from blowing them around.

Someone in the baker's room let out a moan.

The insurance salesman tiptoed back to the door. He opened it a crack and saw Mr. Beránek sitting on the cot pulling at his mustache and shaking his head. Suddenly he jumped up and, taking down the other shovel from the wall, cried out, "That guy had the same angel eyes!" And with a short running start he smashed the shovel into smithereens against the opposite wall.

The insurance man ran into the shop, and before he could close the door he heard Mr. Beránek hollering in the hallway, "This time I'm going to Prague. Horsewhip in hand!"

Mr. Beránek looked both ways to make sure no tram was coming and then stepped into the street to get a better look at the building number. "This is it," he said with great satisfaction, and went inside. There was a plaque on the wall with a sign that said *Small Businessmen's Insurance Company—Sixth Floor.* There was another sign on the elevator door that said *Out of Order.*

Mr. Beránek was in ecstasy. "They know I'm coming and they want to wear me out. But I could fly up twenty flights like an angel and still have strength enough to tear them all to shreds!" And he ran up the stairs, two at a time.

He stopped at the fourth floor. Two old men were sitting on the stairs wiping their foreheads with their handkerchiefs. They were completely and utterly exhausted.

"Small businessmen?" asked the baker.

They nodded, and one of them replied, "How could you tell?"

"Those tortured faces," said Mr. Beránek. "By the way, when you finally get up there and you hear a battle cry, that'll be me cutting them down to size." And having threatened the future victims with his walking stick, he started nimbly up the stairs again, two at a time.

Bursting into the office, he stroked his beard and demanded, "Where's the director?"

The young man in the office had been cutting up a blood sausage. Now he opened a desk drawer and raked all the pieces into it. Then he began paring an onion and finally, squinting his eyes, he said, "I will announce you immediately. What seems to be the trouble?"

"I saved up all my money to buy beechwood, and your insurance man got it all out of me." And to make his point, he banged his walking stick across the desk.

Blinded by tears, the young official stretched out his hands and began fumbling around on the desk. "You almost broke my pepper shaker." He raked the onion slices into the drawer with his fingers, sprinkled the blood sausage with pepper, and leaned down until he was completely out of sight. When he appeared again, he was holding a bottle of vinegar. He tenderly sprinkled a few drops of it into the drawer.

"Won't it leak out?" asked Mr. Beránek.

"Not at all," said the official with a smile. "It has a tin bottom." And while rocking and then shaking the drawer, he added, "It has to be well mixed. Now, what was it you wanted?"

"To see the director," said Mr. Beránek.

"Right away," said the young man and, opening up a pocket knife, he cut himself a slice of blood sausage and began chewing it with great relish. "The drawer where I keep the sausage is labeled 'Meats and Poultry,'" he said with his mouth full, pointing at one of the drawers. "The drawer labeled 'Recreational Facilities' is where I have my books and my harmonica. And this drawer here, the one labeled 'Trash,' is where I keep official documents. Good system, eh? But there was something you wanted," he said, getting up.

"I came to see the director," answered Mr. Beránek, putting his walking stick in the corner.

The official went into a room with an upholstered door, and when he came back he speared a piece of sausage with the tip of his knife, pointed it in the direction of the padded door, and said, "You are expected."

Inside the office at a desk partially concealed by the leaves of an enormous potted palm sat an utterly self-satisfied, complacent, heavy-set man, looking as if he had been expecting to see none other than Mr. Beránek. He offered him a chair and said by way of welcome, "Come in, come in. Sit yourself down. Make yourself at home." But Mr. Beránek refused.

"What's this?" the director asked jovially. "You have a bone to pick with us? You are angry? What have we done to you? Tell us."

And with one eye on the gigantic palm leaf that hovered over the director like an umbrella, the baker told the story of how a handsome young man had come and hypnotized him with his blue eyes and how he had signed the application form in a daze, how he had later read all the small print on the back page and written a letter beginning, "Dear Dirty Bastards, Sons of Bitches, and Murderers," and how another one of their angel-eyed insurance agents had come and talked him out of canceling the policy, and so he had signed a statement saying his complaint had been taken care of. . . . "But my complaint still stands! I want my money back because I need it for my beechwood!"

The director smiled and nodded. "Is that all? Then we'll just strike you from our rolls. After all, small businessmen's pensions are voluntary." He stood up, turned around, thumbed through the files and, when he found what he had been looking for, dropped the folder on the desk with contempt. He sat down and said seriously, "Dear Mr. Beránek. You do not trust us, and although we are terribly grieved, there is nothing we can do. We will have to drop you from our rolls. According to our regulations, however, it is our duty to inform you that you are giving up a great opportunity . . . because—God forbid—what if you should meet with this?" He got up again and pointed to the wall, which was covered with large framed photographs. "Come over here and have a look." And the director tapped his finger on a picture of an organ grinder with a monkey, begging in the street. Mr. Beránek blanched at the sight. The director led him on to the next one, a group of miserable senile old men sitting on a bench in front of a poorhouse. When the picture had had time to register, the director said, "Mr. Beránek, when your precious hands are no longer able to work, who is going to give you anything? Have you ever thought about that? You're a man, aren't you?"

Softly the baker said, "I was wounded in the war."

"There now, you see?" responded the director. "And when you look around, what do you notice on the walls of our office? Just take a look. Pictures of burned-out businesses, businesses stricken by storms or floods. And you are at an age when starting again from scratch is all but impossible, be honest with yourself. Now come and take a look at this showcase. These are clippings from all sorts of newspapers, and . . . and what do they deal with? Accidents, murders, suicides, and bankruptcies with tragic endings. What's that you're reading now?" he asked. "Read it aloud."

And Mr. Beránek read hoarsely, "'Blacksmith's Widow Commits Suicide in Cesspool.'"

"And the next one?"

"'Shopkeeper Cuts Throat with Scythe.'"

"That will suffice," called out the director from a large file cabinet across the room. "We've got thousands like those in here." And crooking his finger, he summoned Mr. Beránek. "Come and see for yourself. If they had had your pension, believe me, they would have avoided all these tragedies, all this grief. But when you don't have the money, there's not much open to you. Only what you see in these pictures, only what you read in these clippings. Now do you really wish to withdraw your application?"

The director took the application form from a folder with "Beránek, Alois" written across it in a fine hand, held it in his fingers, looked the baker in the eyes, and waited for a sign. "Shall I tear it up?" he repeated.

Mr. Beránek looked along the wall, and what he saw staring back at him was those old men in front of the poorhouse and a small shop burned to the ground except for the sign out front. He looked over in the direction of the showcase and saw the sensational headlines. And shaking his head, he whispered, "No, don't. Now I realize that small businessmen need insurance just as much as factory and office workers. . . . Everyone does. . . ."

The director returned the application form to the dossier, sat down under his palm leaf, and folded his hands. "That's why we're here. For you and you alone. At times people need to be saved from themselves, even against their will. Mr. Beránek, it was a pleasure talking to you." And he reached out the tips of his moist fingers for Mr. Beránek to shake.

When Mr. Beránek came out of the director's office, the two

men he had met on the stairs were waiting in front of the padded door, looking at him intently. The young official also lifted his head to have a look at Mr. Beránek's face. Mr. Beránek barely made his way to a chair and sat down. He was as pale as if he had just fallen off a cliff. His mustache was drooping, and his arms hung down between his knees almost to the floor.

"Well, did you knock his teeth in?" asked one of them. But the baker's only response was to stand up, reach over to the corner for his walking stick, lean all his weight on it, and make a slow exit.

After two flights he sat down and rested his head on the finely hewn lily blossom of the art nouveau banister. Just then someone ran into the building and came bounding up the stairs, two at a time. As he leaped past the baker, he called out, "Wait till they hear what I have to tell them! They won't forget me for a long time to come!" And from the floor above he leaned down over the banister and yelled, "A long, long time!" And on he went, his leaps and bounds growing less and less audible until they disappeared altogether and the door of the insurance office slammed behind him.

Mr. Beránek came out onto the square. The square boasted a church with a fountain alongside it. At the center of the fountain stood a sculpture of intertwined fish with water spurting out of each of their mouths. First Mr. Beránek stood and looked at the bubbling water, then he wet his hands in it and dabbed it on his temples, then he laid aside his walking stick, cupped his hands, filled them with the fountain's freshness, and uncupped them over his face. And finally he leaned over the edge and let the water fall on the back of his neck. People stopped to watch, and within a quarter of an hour a policeman came up, gave him a shake or two, and asked, "What are you doing?" Then he caught a glimpse of the baker's face, and added, "Say, are you feeling all right?" Mr. Beránek punched his fist into his open palm and cried out, "They've all got angel eyes!" and stuck his head back under the cool stream of water.

A DULL AFTERNOON

Just after noon a young man—no, he was more of a kid—walked into our neighborhood bar. Nobody knew who he was or where he'd come from. Anyway, he sat down at the table under the compressor and ordered three packs of cigarettes and a beer. Then he opened up this book he had with him, and from then on all he did was read, drink, and smoke. His fingers were all yellow, probably from smoking each cigarette down to where it burned him. Now and then he'd feel around on the tablecloth for a cigarette, light it off the old butt, and puff away. But never for a second did he lift his eyes from his book.

For a while nobody paid any attention to him, because it was just before a soccer game, and the place was packed with the pregame regulars, all dressed up and raring to go—full of spirit for whatever team they were rooting for. They kept straightening their backs as if their coats didn't fit, puffing out their chests, and striking poses with their hands in their pockets. And standing there at the counter downing their last beers, they argued over whether their team would win four-one or five-one.

Then out they streamed, laughing and strutting so that you could tell from three blocks off that they were on their way to the game. When they got to the movie theater at the corner they all turned and waved back at the glass doors, where two

49

heads nodded back. One head belonged to old Jupa, whose doctor had made him cut out soccer after he had two heart attacks in the stands, and the other one—it belonged to the bartender, and he couldn't go because he ran the place. The soccer fans held up their hands, gesticulating. By this time they had reached a sign reading *No Burials on Sunday*, the current attraction at our local movie house. But if you looked out the glass doors of our beer place, what you saw was *Burials on Sunday*, because the corner of the building jutted out a little in the direction of the street and covered up the *No*. They were a happy bunch; anyone could tell they had the game all sewed up. Soon they were just tiny specks at the end of our long street.

They missed their streetcar; it rolled past them, its three cars transformed into three red stripes. So they turned around one more time, waved again . . . and then crossed over onto the island in the middle of the street. . . .

At three o'clock the bartender pushed a button, and the compressor motor on the wall above that kid—he was still reading away—the motor started up and a red light came on. The bartender purposely dropped a cracked stein from as high as he could reach, and even though it hit the floor like a cannon ball, that guy just kept on reading. There was even a smile on his face. The bartender waved his hands in front of the kid's eyes but they never left the book. All he did was grin. "He can't hear, he can't see, he's halfway through his second pack of cigarettes, and I'm about to bring him beer number five. I wonder when he's going to take his little trip over to the john? What is this generation coming to?"

Old man Jupa, who was sitting over by the other wall, facing the kid, made a gesture of despair and shook his head as if to say, "What's the use of talking?"

Then in came someone else no one had ever seen before. A slightly humpbacked, gray-haired little guy carrying a pot of sauerkraut. A pot of sauerkraut on a Sunday afternoon! He ordered a beer and put the pot down in front of him—so he wouldn't forget it, I guess. He rubbed his hands together and looked out the door into the street.

Old man Jupa couldn't take it any longer. "What is this generation coming to anyway? I just wonder what that pipsqueak is reading. I bet it's pornography or some kind of thriller. That's what it is—a sleazy detective story. What a deadhead! Everyone else goes to the game, but His Excellency just sits and reads. Disgusting!"

All in all, he wasn't at all bad-looking. He was wearing the kind of sweater only a mother or a girl friend could knit, the kind that weighs a good twenty-five pounds. He had a red bandana around his neck with a well-made knot; it was like those bandanas bricklayers and village musicians used to wear, tied with a knot as small as a jelly bean. And his head, bent over the book, played up a shock of shiny black hair that looked as if it'd just been doused in motor oil.

The bartender squatted on his heels and looked the boy in the face from below. When he'd had his fill, he stood up and said, "I'll be damned if that guy isn't actually crying!" And he pointed to the tears that had begun to fall all over the page—drip, drop, drip—like beer from the tap.

Well, that made old man Jupa furious. "What a bastard! No wonder we don't have any soccer players! Strong as an ox, and he blubbers like a baby! Disgusting!" And he spit on the floor with great gusto.

The little man who'd brought in the pot of sauerkraut opened his hands and said, "It's all on account of the young people having no ideals. When I was his age I was out on the field. Merz, the famous center forward, had taken a bad spill, and the best center forward of all time, Karel Koželuh, had to go in for him. Johnny Dick, our coach, said to me, 'You take over inside left.' So even though I had trained to play outside right,

I started my career playing inside left. One time, though, Johnny Dick waved a telegram at me across the field and yelled, 'You're in luck. Our outside right is out.' So I finally did get a chance to play outside right."

The little man looked up at old man Jupa, who had the reputation of being an expert, and Jupa said, "Then you must have known Jimmy too, the back who played with Kuchynka."

"Sure I knew him. But Jimmy was his first name. Do you happen to remember his last name?"

All of a sudden you could've heard a pin drop. Jupa had frozen. Then with a grin the little man started up again. "How could you know, anyway? His name was Jimmy Ottaway, and he was English and a crackerjack player."

"What about Kanhäuser?" snapped Jupa.

But the little guy came back with a gesture that showed in no uncertain terms what he thought of our Jupa. "What are you bringing Kanhäuser into the picture for? He didn't start playing with us until '24!"

By this time the kid was feeling around for another cigarette. He lit it off the old butt and shook his yellow fingers for a few seconds—he must have burned himself—but he never let up reading. And now he was laughing, laughing like a hyena, laughing until he was weak.

Old man Jupa jumped up, banged his fist down hard on the table right next to the book, yelled, "Why, you dirty brat, you! Nobody's going to laugh at me!" and went back to his seat.

The boy was so caught up in what he was reading he had broken out into a sweat, so he wiped off his forehead, loosened the bandana, and rolled up the sleeves of his sweater. He was enjoying the book so much that in a burst of high spirits he banged his fist on the table—and so hard that everything took a leap. The bartender was just bringing him another beer.

"You're not the only one here, pipsqueak," the bartender screamed into his ear. "Keep your little tricks to yourself."

So anyway, the young guy—he was still reading and still chuckling away—felt his way up to the glass of beer, took it out of the bartender's hand, and managed to take a deep drink without moving his eyes off the page.

"Beer number six, cigarette number twenty-one," said the bartender in disgust. "What a generation they're going to make, let me tell you. Christ, if he was my son I'd tear that cigarette out of his mouth, even if his whole chin came with it," he yelled, demonstrating on himself how he'd rip off half the kid's face. "But if I want to teach him a lesson, the smart aleck would have the police on my back in two seconds flat!"

Then, to punctuate his statement, he punched the compressor button. The red light went out.

By now Jupa had regained his composure, and he turned to the little man and said, "People who know something about soccer say that only Bican at the height of his career was up to playing with the Real Club."

The little man pushed his pot of sauerkraut to the middle of the table and said, "Oh no! Bican never had the creativity a center forward needs. The only player who would have been up to the real Club was Karel Koželuh. Koželuh had a feeling for team play. And why? Because he played outside left to my outside right. That's why." Then he pulled the pot back to the edge of the table, fished out some sauerkraut with the tips of his fingers, raised the limp little sheaf above his head, opened his mouth, and dropped it in. As he munched, he offered some to Jupa. "Help yourself. It's good for you." But all he got for his pains was a face that clearly said, "Anything but sauerkraut. I can never keep it down." Old man Jupa had begun to look awfully small and awfully miserable.

In the meanwhile the kid—his eyes still glued to the book—had stood up. Nobody'd ever have guessed how tall he was. They don't make them much taller. And the way he held that book of his, you'd think he'd never done anything in his life but hold books like that. He pushed back his chair like a count and then stood stock still in the middle of the room. There must have been some magic in what he was reading. Then he made his way over to the door at the other end of the room with *Rest Rooms This Way* painted on it, opened the door as if he'd done it a thousand times before, and disappeared into our old clubroom. (The clubroom used to have a showcase with our pennants and cups, from the time when you could still get a good game of soccer going in our part of Prague, but now it was being used to store crates of beer and soft drinks.)

Anyway, the bartender had just enough time to say, "What a nut," and point to the closing door, when suddenly we heard a loud crash of bottles followed by a soft tinkling of glass. He threw open the door for all to see, and what they saw was that young punk stumbling his way through an ocean of empty bottles, and—get this—his book still planted firmly in front of his face. Finally he got to the next door. He felt around for the doorknob, turned it, and went into the men's room.

The bartender tiptoed up to the door, opened it a crack, and peeked in. Then he closed it again, crossed through the clubroom, came back into the main room, and said mournfully, "What an awful sight. Picture him—standing there pissing away, and with the other hand he's holding the book—and reading! And that cigarette dangling from his lower lip. No, I've never seen anything like it. I've been serving beer for thirty years now, and never have I seen the likes of it. Maybe I'm wrong, I don't know," and he shook his head, "but this generation will be the death of us."

Jupa asked the little man suspiciously whether he had ever played international ball. "Of course," he answered. "Man, did I have a stroke of hard luck in Stockholm once. I get this beautiful pass, see! So I close my eyes and sidekick it. But the Swedish center half stuck his foot out, and that was the last thing I remembered. Later, in the hospital, Kuchynka told me he heard the bone crack three times and could almost see the stars. I didn't break the leg, though, just tore off the knee-cap. You should have seen how it swelled up. It's a good thing we had a real specialist in Prague—our own Johny Madden."

At this point the young guy came back, reading and smoking and making what looked like treble clefs in the air with his cigarette. He leaned against the doorjamb with the toes of one foot resting on the floor and the heel straight up and down. After a while he started back to his seat, but when he got to the center of the room he stopped and wrinkled up his fore-head, as if something he'd read had given him a terrible shock. Then he shook his head, and tears as big as hailstones began to fall. Some of them fell on the back of old man Jupa's hand, and Jupa jumped up and shouted, "Nobody's going to cry over me!" Anyway, when the kid finally got back to his place, he practically collapsed into the chair.

Old man Jupa was furious. "Who ever heard of such a thing! Johny Madden a knee specialist. Johny Madden was a coach!" He looked up at the bartender, and the bartender be-gan to laugh.

The guest, who was just about to drop another sheaf of sauerkraut into his mouth, jerked his head forward, threw the sauerkraut back into the pot, and said, "You can't be very up on things if you don't know about the miracles Johny Madden used to perform on sprained ankles. Why, all the ballerinas used to go to him. He had a ballerina in there with him the time they brought me in. 'Don't worry. We'll have you fixed up in no time,' he said to me while he massaged the dancer. Johny Madden . . . he was a great coach too of course. . . ." And he picked up the sauerkraut again, threw his head back, and dropped it into his mouth.

Now old man Jupa had a reputation for being an expert, and he was fit to be tied. He stroked his bald head in self-pity and kept saying, "Impossible, impossible," to himself. He seemed to have begun to shrink as soon as he started talking to the little guy. His neck was gone; his head sat right on his shoulders.

The bartender tried to save the day by pushing the button on the master board. It lit up the red light and started the compressor motor growling. "Sometimes I wonder," he said, "where those punks get their money. When I was a kid, you were a millionaire if you had enough for a few beers!"

"Forget about him," old man Jupa chimed in. "He'll end up in reform school anyway. Just look at him. Four o'clock in the afternoon, this game could knock our team out of first place, and all our noble friend here can do is sit and chain-smoke and get sloshed. Where else is he going to end up but jail? He'll probably go and murder a cigar store lady."

"Hey, waiter!" the kid shouted. And don't think he looked up from his book, either. No, all he did was motion toward himself and rub his thumb and forefinger together to show he was ready to pay.

"Did you see that? Did you hear that? I'm afraid to say anything to him. If only Comenius could see this. . . ." He shook his head and added up the beers. "That'll be seventeen crowns."

The young guy took out a fistful of bills from his pocket the way the little guy picked up the sauerkraut from his pot. Then he separated out two ten-crown bills and put them at the far end of the table, like a pianist reaching for those real low notes. Then he made a "Do what you see fit with the change" gesture with his hand, crumpled up the rest of the money, and stuck it in his pocket like a handkerchief. But the bartender laid down a three-crown note next to the book and said to him, "You can keep your change. I'll have no dealings with a jailbird."

They watched the boy put out his cigarette in the ashtray. He was as careful as if he was ringing a doorbell. Then he felt around on the tablecloth for another cigarette, put it in his mouth, took out his matches, struck one, set fire to the three-crown note, and lit the cigarette with it—all without lifting his eyes from the book. As he inhaled, he waved the flaming bank note in the air, and when it finally began to burn him, he dropped it into the ashtray all twisted and black. It sat there like a piece of carbon paper. Then he leaned his forehead up against his thumb and index finger, looking as much like a monument as a person can.

The bartender spat, bent down, and whispered, "Nothing is holy any more. There was a time when people would climb a fence to catch a feather the wind had blown away, and what does this juvenile delinquent do? He uses money to light his cigarettes! And you can be sure he didn't earn it for himself. How old do you think he is, anyway? Twenty-one? What will he be like when he's thirty? Why, he'll set the whole place on fire."

Then old man Jupa started in again. "What about František Svoboda?"

The little gray-haired guy couldn't have looked more patronizing. "You mean Franci? A great passer and a real tank. But he can't compare with Koželuh. The way Franci passed to Zámora—why, to this very day Zámora jumps out of bed when he dreams of that bomb coming at him. The trouble was, Franci loved picking fights. If you'd ever gone to soccer matches, you'd have remembered his battles with the Hungarians . . . Ferencvárosi Torna Egysilét. Turay, who was known for his brutality, and Toldi, that two-hundred-twenty-five-pound giant, both running wild, and right there in the thick of it—our tank Svoboda. But when it comes to teamwork, Koželuh was impossible to beat. And why? Because he played outside left to my outside right. You follow me?"

Old man Jupa, who couldn't have been more than a few years younger than the little guy, had shrunk so much during the last few minutes that his head was on a level with his stein; all he had to do was tip it a little and he was in business.

The sun beat down. The right-hand side of the street was steeped in bluish shadows, while the roofs on the left-hand side were just barely holding up under the weight of the light. And the *Burials on Sunday* sign—the come-on, in today's lingo —was ablaze with iridescent paint. It was like the light reflecting off hundreds of pocket mirrors. At the end of the street, where you could see right through the trams—there were so few people riding them—paraded a steady stream of walkers in all shapes and sizes, with a baby carriage thrown in here and there for good measure. The kid stood up from under the compressor motor. His face was striped from the light coming in off the street. His eyes were still glued to the book. And taking his coat off the hook, he put one arm through a sleeve and then stood there in that ridiculous-looking pose—one arm in, one arm out—like a scarecrow in a cabbage patch, and kept right on reading.

The little guy added up his own bill, put down the money next to his glass, and picked up the pot of sauerkraut. Old man Jupa stood up, grabbed that pot like it was a life preserver, and shouted, "Are you trying to tell me we play lousy soccer?" And as he shouted, he shook the pot.

But the little guy, who stood opposite him, had held onto it and was shaking it along with Jupa—so hard he almost tore Jupa's arm out of its socket. "Cut the crap now, will you? One day I pivoted twice in a row, and before you knew it the whole team was shouting, 'Play that ball, or you're out of the game on Sunday!' Take Borovička, for example. He's got all the technical know-how but no sense of team play. Or Kučera—a great player, but he hogs the whole show. No, to the best of my knowledge—and I'd swear it on a stack of Bibles—the best soccer ever was played by . . . the best soccer player of all times was Karel Koželuh. And you know why? Because he played outside left to my outside right." And he pulled the pot right out of the hands of a very disgruntled Jupa.

Then he looked out into the street. Over by the coming attractions pictures in front of the movie theater stood this real stacked broad sucking on a hard candy and looking at the pictures. "What a woman!" exclaimed the little man, in a trance. "God, what a woman! Now that's what I call a woman! And you know what she needs. Of course there aren't any real men around nowadays to give it to her. No man today can even begin to understand a woman like that. What a woman!" And shaking his head, he read into that woman just what he had been talking about. Suddenly there she was—twirling her bag and sucking her candy and heading straight for us. When she was all but at the glass door—it even got a little darker inside— she turned again and showed us all her beautiful curves in profile and walked past. "That woman is my ideal," said the little man, and he tucked the pot under his arm and set out after her like a sleepwalker or something.

Anyway, the kid finally pulled on the other sleeve, and—still holding the book in both hands—he spit out the last butt and ground it into the floor with his shoe. Then he put one hand on the glass door, shoved it open, and disappeared. Left the door open and disappeared.

"And not a word the whole time he was here," said the bartender. He just couldn't keep himself from going outside and yelling, "You good-for-nothing pipsqueak!" after the kid, and slamming the door real hard.

The glass gave out a suspicious rattle, and the bartender froze. "Jupa, I'm scared to turn around. Did I break it?" But Jupa shook his head no.

So there they sat, looking out the glass door. A crowd of people buying tickets began to form in front of the movie house. Old man Jupa looked up at the iridescent *No Burials on Sunday* sign and spit. "What an idiotic sign. Let's hope it's not a bad omen for our team." The bartender was nervous by nature, and the kid with the book hadn't exactly helped, so he started brush-cleaning glasses and holding them up to the light to make sure they were clean, just so he wouldn't be the first one to see the soccer crowd turn the corner.

Suddenly old man Jupa cried out, "Here they come!"

The first one to round the corner was Mr. Hurych, followed almost immediately by the others. They were all bedraggled and hunched over; they all looked withered and small, as if they'd gotten drenched and their clothes had shrunk. Right under the *No Burials on Sunday* sign Mr. Hurych tore off his hat, threw it down on the sidewalk, and started jumping on it. The others tried to console him. Then, just to make it absolutely clear how much he was suffering, Mr. Hurych took off his overcoat, threw it down, and started jumping on it too.

"There's something funny going on here," said old man Jupa. "Must have been a tie." And when he saw Mr. Hurych reaching for the doorknob, he opened the door for him himself. Well, Hurych fell in a heap on the first seat he came to and just sat there, looking out into space. The rest of the crowd came in and waited to see what he would do. Finally he picked himself up, took off his jacket, threw it down on the floor, collapsed back onto the bench, and said, "All eleven. No exceptions. Send all eleven to the mines!" And he pointed off in the direction where he figured the nearest mines to be.

Old man Jupa went over to the glass door and looked out. He didn't even notice that the beautiful woman, the one with the twirling handbag, had turned back onto our street, and that the outside right with the pot of sauerkraut was still sleepwalking ten feet behind her. She went into the movie theater, and there he was, right behind her.

So anyway, here was old man Jupa standing in the glass door with his arms stretched out like Christ on the cross. And if anyone had happened to look at him from the side, they would have seen tiny tears making their way down his cheeks. But by then the bartender had begun passing around a tray of fortifying brandy.

EVENING COURSE

I'd been standing around the corner for quite some time when a motorcycle finally turned from Marián Square and made its way in my direction. It was a Jawa 250 with double handle-bars. The instructor slid gracefully off the rear seat and pulled out a cigarette with his numb fingers. Before lighting it, he cast a reproachful glance at his pupil, who was still trying to kick the machine into neutral.

"Still can't get it, can you! He still hasn't got it," grumbled the instructor, his cigarette bouncing up and down between his lips. "You didn't make a very good show of yourself today, you know. Those intersections—awful! And turn off your lights! Now, quick—what are the rules about right of way?"

"It's like this, Mr. Fořtík," said the young man, running his fingers through his crew cut. "I took the course back in January, and here it is September. I must have a block or something. I know the stuff, all right. It's just that I can't seem to spit it out."

"But what about the test? You have to have everything at your finger tips. Sit down and learn it by heart, damn it. As soon as you get home from work, pick up the rules and start memorizing, understand?"

"I understand. But when I get home I go right to sleep."

"Well, go ahead, take your nap. But sooner or later you've

got to wake up. And then pick up those rules. It's only a few pages, damn it! What do you do when you wake up?"

"Read. And do I have a terrific book! *Bestial Dr. Quartz and the Fair Zanona.* Nick Carter. Man, what a story! Want to borrow it?"

"Look, I'm still in a good mood. Don't spoil it. Okay, you're done with *Fair Zanona.* What then?"

"Oh, later in the evening is out of the question, Mr. Fořtík. You ought to see my girl. There's a machine for you. Beautiful balance, not an ounce of excess baggage. Those streamlined valves. That perfect cylinder. And what a camshaft! The guys really flip when we zoom by."

"So you've been out without a license, eh? Just keep it up."

"What do you expect, Mr. Fořtík? I started lessons in January with a cycle waiting out back in the shed. I held out till July, but then—it was a Sunday, and there was nobody home —I dragged the full-length mirror out of my room into the yard, and in full regalia I rode straight up to the mirror just to see how good I looked. I stared at myself in that mirror till I couldn't take it any more. Out I went. And you can bet your bike I left half the poor saps on the road choking on my exhaust."

"Okay, okay. You're just wasting your breath and my time. Though, by the way, you might very well have wrecked the hell out of the machine. Okay, now you've dropped your girl off, you go home, it's nice and quiet, and you pick up the rules. What else is there to do so late at night?"

"Late at night? That's when I really start moving. I flip the dial to Munich or Luxemburg and listen to those black guys go wild. Electric banjo, electric guitar, trumpet—with bass and piano—just for the beat. How about coming over sometime? Bing Crosby and Grace Kelly, Eartha Kitt, the black nightingale, and Louis Satchmo Armstrong. The way they go at it, it's enough to break your heart."

"Okay, okay. I'm done with my cigarette. We might just drive out to your place sometime. I could even stick around for a little jazz. But at this point I'm still your teacher, and we've got our last lesson coming up on Saturday, and before you turn that key you're going to rattle off the whole book for me. One slip, and I'm not climbing aboard. Though you'll be a good driver in any case; you haven't got any phobias. What do you do for a living?"

"I'm a bookbinder."

"All right, I'll sign your card this time, but remember: next time, the book, and by heart! Seriously."

"I'll be cramming it all week, don't worry. Just for you I will. If I can keep from going off my rocker, you'll have it all by heart. Thanks and good night."

"Good night, you little so-and-so," muttered the instructor under his breath, and turned to me. "You're Hrabal, right? You have your own machine too?"

"Yes, I do, Mr. Fořtík."

"Say, aren't you turning gray? How come you've decided to take up the cycle so late in life?"

"I had no other choice, Mr. Fořtík. My legs have been giving me trouble, and since I've always enjoyed walking around and looking at things, I figured one of the CZ beauties would do the trick. Across the fields, through the woods, along the water . . . Where I come from, the water smells like fresh-broken reeds."

"Hm. You talk a pretty picture. Let me have another smoke. I'm cold again. So this is your first time out."

"Oh no! I've ridden motorcycles before, only it was always my father who drove. I sat behind. As far back as I can remember. Our first cycle was a Laurin—the kind you had to crank—with a sidecar for my mother and brother. By the time we'd cranked her up enough so she'd catch, we were too weak to hop on, me and my father."

"You know, even I can't remember that far back. . . . Anyway, let's say you're taking your test. Why is oil used for lubrication?"

"Oil film. Viscosity."

"Fine. And what is compression ratio?"

"The ratio of the maximum to the minimum volume of the piston of an internal combustion engine during a complete stroke."

"Even better, even better. But mark my words: it's those knuckleheads without a bit of theory behind them who are going to drive around like gods, and you, you're sure to take a spill sooner or later. But don't let that get you down, because you won't know how to drive till you've got 'er wide open, you take a bad spill—and live to tell the tale. That's when you'll start putting some real mileage on that bike of yours. You know, your father was a pioneer. Does he still get out there?"

"You bet he does, Mr. Fořtík. It's all we ever talk about at home. But now he's switched over to cars. I wouldn't be surprised if he pictures heaven as an eternity of tinkering on a huge meadow of junked cars, with St. Peter handing out tool kits at the Pearly Gates. But when I was a boy, it was murder! Dad liked the feel of the wind in his hair, and Mother, like every other mother, was a little weak in the nerve department. But he would soothe her with 'A little breeze will do wonders for you,' and off we'd go. Then, once we'd passed a few buggies, he would forget all about her nerves and crouch down over the handlebars and cry, 'Targo Florio!' and there was no holding him back. Through the haze I could see Mother clutching my brother, squeezing the hell out of him and screaming, 'Franci, Franci, for heaven's sake, Franci,' all the way. Dad never let up. That was when cotton raincoats were all the rage, and Dad's always used to balloon up. It gave him a hump that reached all the way back to me."

"You mean you went that fast along the dirt roads they had

then? What about your springs? They must've been in awful shape."

"And how! Especially for me. We had double springs back where I sat. Special ones. The passenger seat was made to order because Dad's boss, who sometimes rode with him, weighed a couple of hundred pounds or more. Take my word for it, Mr. Fořtík, the only time I got to see any of the countryside was when we were just starting up or when we stopped for repairs. Otherwise the tears in my eyes made the landscape look fuzzy, and the woods and fields just jounced by."

"Hm. So your father was a real hero."

"To us kids he was, but not to Mom. Instead of admiring the sights when we got to where we were going, I'd have to throw up, and Mom would be draped over the sidecar, gulping down pills and moaning, 'Why did I ever come along? Why did I ever come along?' All Mom could see in our outings was the hospital or the cemetery looming in the distance; all Dad saw was a direct route to Targo Florio Racetrack. Almost before the beautiful countryside could soothe us back to normal it was time for a repeat performance—the trip home. Dad would promise Mom, he would swear up and down, that he was going to drive in a manner befitting a family outing, but by the time fifteen minutes had rolled by the open road got to him again, and off we would fly through the countryside like ghosts. It's the only fun Dad ever got out of life."

"Okay. I'm through with my smoke now. Let's get going," said the instructor.

I pulled the motorcycle off the stand and kicked it back.

"Let's go over it all one more time, now, Hrabal. First you turn the key in the starter. This machine shifts a little different from your CZ."

"But I don't drive it. I don't have a license."

"I realize that, but let's say I'm talking academically. Now then, first is up; second, third, and fourth—down. When you go from one to the next, you're best off just popping it in there. What about your lights?"

"Are you set, Mr. Fořtík?"

"All set, but you see? She's died on you. Give her more gas, rev her up a little. Then let the clutch out easy. Now try it again. . . . It's not going to work that way, Hrabal."

"Oh yes. I see. I'm still in first," I said, blushing. And kicking it into neutral with my instep, I finally started it up. The motor gave out a roar, and suddenly, even though there was no one in sight, I could feel all of Prague watching me. When I shifted into first, the world began to spin.

Mr. Fořtík leaned forward and whispered, "Relax, Hrabal. Give her some gas. Now look back to make sure no one is coming. Give a hand signal to show you're pulling out. Now shift . . . good . . . and take a left. Second, put her into second! Now brake 'er a little and look around. We're coming to a tri-angular road sign; that means look sharp. Now take a right down Kaprova. Don't forget to signal. Stick your hand out more. More! You look like you're scratching your knee or fixing a loose garter. Now we've lost speed, so put her into first . . . now second . . . third . . . A tap of the heel will do. And now, past the New Town Hall and signal a left turn. Watch out for streetcar tracks, especially after it rains, or first thing you know we'll be smeared all over the street. Now left up Dlouhá. Make sure nothing's coming in our direction and there's no streetcar behind us. Good, and now take a right. Tell me, did you and your father ever crack up that Laurin?"

"The BMW 57, not the Laurin. But Dad did crack up the Laurin several times on his own. When Mom couldn't take those long trips any more, we'd take the train to wherever we were going and Dad would meet us there on the cycle. The only thing was, he never made it. Once when we had gone ahead to Brno he came in on the train the next day, his arm in a sling and his head all bandaged up. But he didn't seem upset at all. In fact, he made a joke of it, telling us how he'd run into a church, straight into the sacristy."

"The sacristy? Now that's something I haven't tried. Never even occurred to me. All right now, you had to drop into first to slow down for that old man. Now turn right. Revoluční is clear. Step on it! More. More! It's a good idea to go heavy on the gas when you're stopped at an intersection. There's nothing as embarrassing as having her die on you at an intersection. Hats off to your father, by the way. Did he keep it up?"

"You bet he did, and the older he got the more reckless he drove. Every ride a race. Another time he was supposed to meet us with a friend. Well, both he and that friend of his showed up on the train. And again they were all bandaged up. Crashed into a team of oxen. As they stepped off the train Dad assured us, announced, happy as could be, 'Just you wait. I'll make it yet.'"

"Put her into first, Hrabal. Take a right and pipe down for a while. This is a tough stretch. Besides, remember that the motorcycle is a mythical beast. The more it bucks you, the more you cling to it. You'll find out for yourself when you're lying in a ditch some night with a broken leg. Not so close to that streetcar. Some jerk'll jump out . . . and besides, what does the book say? How are you supposed to drive?"

"At a safe distance, one that will allow me to stop without difficulty."

"Very good, Hrabal. What's your damn hurry anyway? Honk! The Powder Tower intersection is hell. I once took a spill here with one of my pupils. He rode onto the tracks, like you did just then, and broke his collarbone. You see, you don't just react to what's already in your way. Be on the lookout at all times. Always keep your eyes open. Look out for people or else it's bam—the end. Of course you've got to be lucky too, but then again you need a bit of luck even if you're only out for a walk around Prague. Now let's turn up Wenceslas

Square. Don't worry about the traffic lights; they're off for the night. Into first, now. Right, the road is clear. Now proceed up the hill in the middle lane. Your father must have had one hell of a time with his Laurin. You ought to put one on his grave as a monument. Quiet, no talking, not now. Watch out for the intersection at Vodičkova. All right. Now we're okay, you can go on. . . ."

"I was just thinking of another one of our excursions—to the spa at Poděbrady. It was summer and we were all decked out in our Sunday best—my brother and I in our sailor suits and Dad in a brand-new, extra-long coat. For a while the coat fluttered in the breeze, but then suddenly it got caught in the back wheel . . ."

"In the *rear* wheel, Hrabal."

"Right. Anyway, as that rear wheel gobbled up his coat, Dad slid back closer and closer to where I was sitting. He tried to reach the gas but the coat kept pulling him down onto his back, and all he could do was grasp out at nothing. Then I started sliding down on my back along with him . . ."

"Fascinating, Hrabal. Don't forget what you were saying, but let's take a right. And don't sit all hunched up like that. Let me straighten you out. There. And now right again, down Ječná. As you were saying . . ."

"So we sailed across a ditch and landed in the middle of a rye field. In those days, cloth was much tougher than it is now. If it had happened more recently, the coat would have ripped in two!"

"Hold it, Hrabal. The intersection at St. Ignác's is a tricky one. There's a hospital on the left, and the ambulances are always going in and out. You'd be better off in second. And try to remember for when you're out on your own that as a rule you're better off staying out of fourth downtown. Look out for the gas stations over there and the Technicum Straight up ahead. And now let's head down to the Vltava."

"Even though Father was practically lying on top of me, we kept going round and round in the field, up to our necks in rye . . ."

"Hold it, Hrabal. You've got to develop a feel for it. Now we'll turn onto the embankment, keep going, past the National Theater, and then all the way back up to where we started out from. Here, let those soldiers pass you. By the sound of it they must be driving a Tatra 111. There, what did I tell you? A one-eleven. And now give her the gas! You've got to make a fast getaway from an intersection. That's the way . . ."

"So anyway, there we were, racing around through the rye, with Dad using his free foot to keep the Laurin on course. All that showed was three heads; Mother had long since fainted and was completely out of the picture. Finally my brother reached out of the sidecar and began testing one lever after another—you know how many there used to be—to the accompaniment of Dad's 'That's not it! No, not that one either!' until he finally hit on the right one and the machine came to a slow stop in the middle of the field. But we sure had trouble disentangling Father from the wheel. Luckily some men working in the field came and cut him free with a scythe. All Dad could make from what was left of the coat was a very short windbreaker. . . ."

"Careful here. You know what? Let's stay out a while longer. Down to the University Law School, and turn right on Pařížská. But watch out for those tracks! So then you bought a BMW, right?"

"Right. Now there was a speed demon. That was back when Tazio Nuvolari was all the rage. We'd go so fast we wouldn't see a thing. It was like being enveloped in a large cloud, pierced from time to time by Father's cry of 'Nuvolari!' Should I go into first?"

"What for? The bridge here is closed. I'll bet he gave that

71

BMW a run for its money. Where did you have your first accident?"

"The BMW had a sidecar on it too, and once, to pass a team of horses, Father gave her the gas, and we got caught on the lynchpin of the cart and made a full turn on its axis. I flew out into a pear tree and broke my collarbone. It was during summer vacation, as a matter of fact, the very first day of vacation; we were on our way to Prague to buy me a hat for my good report card. Father flew over the handlebars and smashed his glasses into his eyebrows. My brother fell out of the sidecar and walked away without a scratch. But Father wanted to shoot himself, then and there, in the street: the blood streaming down his face made him think he had lost his sight. 'I'm blind!' he screamed. We ran and draped ourselves around him. We wanted him to shoot us too. It's a good thing there were people around. They carted me off to a doctor. He put me into a cast. Where to now? Down Sanytrova?"

"That's right. But what about your father?"

"I was sitting in a roadside café, when who should turn the corner but my father and brother and a mudguard from the sidecar. Underneath his bandaged head Father was laughing away. 'Quite a crash, wasn't it?' he called out to me."

"Be careful here, Hrabal. I once had a pupil give her the gas near the Klementinum when it was wet, the way it is now, and I had no choice but to take the spill along with him. That was a good hand signal. And now let's turn back. Keep going, put her in first . . . and now we'll turn around. Keep your foot off the ground; I could easily kick it. Cut the gas, put her in neutral, and turn the key in the starter. A shame this is our only time out together. And how did your mother feel about it?"

"She was on her way to feed the chickens when we rode through the gate: the gauze and plaster brotherhood, complete with torn-off mudguard. Mom stood holding the tray with chicken feed, and Dad grinned at her. 'Now that was a really fine, a great ride!' he said. Well, Mother collapsed. Out cold. The feed scattered among the chickens, and the chickens fell to."

"Think I'll have a smoke. And let me tell you, your father was a true bard and lived a worthy life. Here, give me your card. I'll sign it for you."

He entered the lesson on my driving-school record and signed his name.

"You know, you and your father have made my day," he said, handing back the card. Then he jumped on the kick starter. "Getting colder, isn't it? My best to your father!"

"I'll be sure to tell him."

Mr. Fořtík touched his forehead in a mock salute and turned on the ignition. And taking advantage of an especially slippery patch in the wet pavement, he made a 180-degree turn on the spot and rattled off in the direction of the Vltava.

THE FUNERAL

"What a nice dream I had last night. I dreamed I was kneeling in the woods in front of a threshing machine when out of nowhere up flew St. Joseph and made a big cross over me. This morning I knew right off I'd put my money on number 19, ice hockey, and number 3, bicycle racing, in the sports lottery, because St. Joseph's saint's day is the 19th of March," said Jarda, buttoning his coat. Just as he was about to tell Pepík about how the sports lottery provided a great incentive to dreams and dream interpretation, a terrible crash followed by a loud clatter and loud cursing cut him short. Jarda and Pepík tumbled into the tarred gully of the pissoir, and as they were picking themselves up, Jarda noticed that a milky piece of broken glass with the number 8 on it had landed beside him.

"Well, what do you know! Mountain climbing! Eight!" he rejoiced.

"But look at my coat," said Pepík, inspecting his sleeves.

"It's a sign from the heavens," rejoiced Jarda, admiring his piece of glass. "Let me tell you, this is the only kind of number worth anything. The kind with fate behind it. Ice hockey and bicycle racing this morning, and now mountain climbing!"

"This suit is going to have to go to the cleaner's," answered Pepík dryly.

They didn't see it until they had come out of the pissoir. A truck had rammed straight into a glass-encased clock that until then had shown the hour to all four cardinal points. The impact of the crash had knocked all four clock faces out onto the pavement and bent the iron base of the clock across the pissoir.

The two friends made their way through the numbers to a policeman who was slipping a preserve-jar rubber band off his memo book. "Do you have any idea how lucky you were? You're okay, aren't you?" he asked.

"Yes."

"And did you see it?"

"No, we only heard it from in there," said Jarda, pointing to the pissoir.

"All right then. You can go," said the policeman, and went over to the driver of the truck, whose hands were trembling so much he was having trouble putting together his papers.

"Mountain climbing! In a week we'll be rich!" said Jarda. He kissed the 8 and then threw it down on the pavement with the rest of the glass.

Pepík looked at his watch and said, "That's all well and good, but let's make sure we don't miss the funeral."

After a while they found the wind so strong that they pretty much had to bend over double to make any headway.

Jarda was all excited. "There's always a bit of magic involved in the lottery. No system is worth beans. I've kept a list of all the winning numbers, and you know, yachting and canoeing haven't come up at all. That lucky Jewish number has come up only once, and unlucky 13—nine times. Your uncle Adolf, the one whose funeral we're going to, he once told me, 'Moles dig holes at odd hours; odd numbers should be lucky.' So we put our money down, and every single number came up even." He stopped to catch his breath.

"There's the secret. You've got to enter into a personal relationship with the numbers. You've got to have a one-for-all-and-all-for-one friendship with them. You almost have to treat them like you would a lover. That's the secret. Take this car, for example. Passing it on our way up the hill, it's nothing but a piece of junk to me, but if I was lucky enough to have it run me over a little, its license plate would have some meaning in my life. But just passing it on the way up the hill . . ."

"Jarda, watch out!" cried Pepík, jumping to one side. A heavy barrel had come loose from a truck that was coming down the hill and had rolled under the wheels of the car on its way up, a few yards from the two of them. A column of yellow dust exploded into the air, followed by a loud crash and the screeching of tires.

Pepík stood by the side of the road and inspected his mourning suit in despair; it was every bit as yellow as the quickly growing yellow cloud out of which Jarda had begun to totter.

"You stupid idiot! What kind of way is that to drive!" yelled Pepík into the cloud, and resumed inspecting his clothes.

"No blasphemy, now," warned Jarda, putting his hand over his friend's mouth. "Remember, it's a sign from the heavens." He pointed to the pillar of yellow dust that the wind had begun to propel across the blackish snow. "By the end of the month we'll have struck it rich," he choked, and then took a walk around the car, which had just emerged from the cloud. He knelt down in the two-foot-deep drift of yellow dust and wiped off the license plate. The wind quickly yellowed it over again. The only way he could read it was to concentrate on individual numbers and give them each a quick wipe.

"Diving!" And then . . . "Horseback riding!" And a final wipe . . . "Gymnastics!"

The wind obscured the license plate with the dust and swept the fine aniline powder under the car and up into the air. The driver still had his hands on the steering wheel, his eyes were closed, and he kept hoping that it was all just a dream, that all he had to do was open his eyes and he would find that nothing he had seen, heard, or felt had in fact occurred. . . . Just as he finally did open them, a Tatra 111 truck sped down the hill, reactivating the dust, which this time coated all the car's windows.

"Gymnastics!" cried out Jarda gleefully.

The owner of the car screwed up his courage and jumped out. "Jesus, my first time on the road!" Then he realized he was standing knee deep in yellow dust and began wringing his hands in despair.

"Excuse me, but I'm afraid to look. What is that under my wheel?" The wrinkles in his forehead ran straight to his ears.

"A two-hundred-pound barrel of aniline," answered Pepík.

"Why, why did I have to take her out today?" he moaned, pressing his yellowing hand to his forehead. "What a scene my wife is going to make! I'm afraid to look. Is there much damage?"

"What about my suit? We're on our way to a funeral. My uncle's," said Pepík with a sigh, but he did go to take a look at the front of the car. "It's not as bad as all that. The left wheel is torn off and the fender has a slight dent in it. And the radiator is smashed in a bit."

"What is my wife going to say?" the driver whined, covering his face with his hands.

"She's not going to sing your praises, that's for sure," said Pepík, looking at his wrist watch after wiping it clean. "But worst of all . . . Do you really want me to tell you?" he asked.

"Go ahead, I can take anything now."

"The whole chassis's out of whack."

"Jesus Christ! Will there be hell to pay!" Out of desperation he climbed back into the car in what was now his yellow coat, unhooked a feather duster that was hanging beside the back window, and began nervously dusting off the car he had taken out for the first time.

A little boy with a sled had come all the way down the almost bare slope to have a look at the car. He picked up a

78

fistful of aniline dust, tugged the car's owner by the sleeve, and asked, "What's this, mister?"

The man let out a shrill cry. "Get away from me. Get out of here or I'll . . . I've only got one set of nerves!" He beat the air ferociously with his many-colored feather duster.

"We'll send you a cop when we get to the top of the hill," said Jarda, and started on his way again, repeating to himself, "Driving . . . Horseback riding . . . Gymnastics . . ."

The wind at the cemetery was blowing so fiercely that the trees' bare branches vibrated like flagpoles. Although next to the chapel a band of chilled-to-the-bone musicians were moving their fingers and puffing out their cheeks, the results were practically nil; as soon as a note came out of an instrument the wind would blow it away. Pepík read the sign with his uncle's name on it and bellowed, "Which way did they go?"

One of the musicians shut his eyes and, without missing a note, pointed his instrument toward an indefinite over there.

"That way?" asked Pepík, pointing, and the musician nodded and went on punching the keys. His gloves had cut-off finger tips.

"Those musicians play like someone writing with a No. 3 pencil," said Jarda with inspiration. "But maybe the wind is whipping those funeral songs up against a wall somewhere on the other side of town and people are wondering where all the funeral music could be coming from. Hey, that must be them now."

"What?" asked Pepík, holding a cupped palm up to his yellow ear.

"That must be them now!" yelled Jarda, and off they went over the gravestones. By the time they got there the service was over. The priest had taken off his biretta and was in the process of sprinkling the grave. The wind was so strong it forced the mourners to hold onto their hats with both hands and carried the holy water off to another grave. The tiny purple acolyte was struggling bravely against the wind's efforts to overturn the crucifix and kept getting slapped in the face by the banners.

"What section is this?" called out Jarda.

"Roman numeral nine."

"Roman numeral what?"

To outshout the gale, Pepík screamed, "Nine, number nine!" at the top of his lungs.

Suddenly there was a lull in the wind, and the entire funeral party turned to witness a completely yellow latecomer shout, "Yachting!"

THE NOTARY

I

Every morning the notary would say his prayers in his family chapel, a room with two stained-glass windows. One of them depicted St. Dionysius, carrying his head around the executioner's block; the other, the messenger returning a chopped-off arm to St. Agatha's corpse.

One morning, kneeling in prayer, he realized with a pang of guilt that he had forgotten to gargle. Finally he made the sign of the cross, stood up, and opened the window.

When his eyes had grown used to the morning sun he looked up, over the blue roofs, to the other side of the river, and treated himself to a few deep breaths of the damp air.

"Grammmaaaall! Grammmaaaall!" cried a child's voice. "Baby Zdeněk is eating dog-do."

The notary stood up on his toes and scanned the courtyard of what had once been a brewery and now had people living in it. A little girl in a red smock and straw hat was pointing at a three-year-old boy who was blissfully sticking something into his mouth.

A thin woman ran out of the laundry room, threw up her hands, and yelled, "God damn you little brats! When am I ever going to get done with the washing!" She grabbed her grandson and shook him over the sewer grating. "You filthy little pig, you! Just wait till Mother comes home. She'll hit you where it hurts!" Then all at once she changed her tactics and with a slap across the face knocked the dog-do out of his mouth. Next she lit into the girl. "What are you staring at? If you don't watch out I'll swat you one too and knock your cross-eyes straight. Here," she added, taking a whistle from the pocket of her blue apron. "Go play in the kitchen, and if anything happens, give a toot on the whistle. With two little gangsters like you, how will I ever get the washing done?" Again she threw up her hands; they were blue from the wash.

The notary closed the window. He went out into the dreary hallway and then straight into the office.

"Good morning, sir," said the young typist, not looking up from the flowers she was watering.

"Good morning, good morning," mumbled the old man, and rubbing his hands together, he added, "And how did we spend yesterday?"

"Well, first I played tennis, and you know what? I lost. I lost to a woman fifteen years older than I am. And I lost by two sets. Isn't that awful?"

"Yes, what a pity," said the notary. "But from what I understand, you're an excellent player."

"Well no, not exactly," she said, blushing. "I still have a long way to go. I just must have been nervous, that's all."

"Because you thought your opponent might beat you?"

"No, not that either. But that's me all over. As soon as something important is at stake I go to pieces and lose everything. You don't know how unhappy it makes me! And it was a club tournament game!"

"Well, you'll win next time. And what else did you do?"

"Well, it was dark by the time I'd had my cry in the locker room, but I decided to go swimming. I got into my bathing suit and swam upstream, as far as the big oak. The moon had come out, a gigantic yellow moon. I climbed up on a rock and splashed my legs in the water and stared down at the ripples and the moon shining yellow in it . . ."

"And then?" asked the notary, raising his eyebrows.

"And then I slipped back down into the water, into the brass-colored water, and swam and swam, round and round in the reflection of the moon, pushing away the metallic paint with my hands. Each time I raised my hand, it came out bronze. You can't imagine the thrill it gave me."

"And what then?"

"Then something gave me a fright."

"Really?"

"Yes," she said, taking her seat at the typewriter. "Guess what I saw coming out of the darkness, the pitch-black darkness of the woods? Three pairs of white bathing trunks."

"Bathing trunks?" asked the old man incredulously.

"That's right. Three pairs of white bathing trunks. So I ducked into the reeds and stayed quiet as a mouse. And they walked right over me across the dam. I could hear everything they said. And you know what they were?"

"No, but I'd like to!"

"Three naked men! They were tan, and they must have had their trunks on when they were out in the sun, and their arms and legs and all the rest of their bodies merged with the shadows, and they were naked. Naked! And I thought at first that those bathing trunks were walking all by themselves." She blushed.

"And did you see everything?"

"Oh yes, everything, absolutely everything. They were three young students. The same age as me."

"That must have been something," said the old man bitterly. "That must really have been something. A young girl, bronze water, and three pairs of white trunks darting in and out among the shadows. Well, and what did you do then?"

"Then I swam back to the club because I heard the three

students diving into the water. Then I dried off and went home."

"And at home?"

"At home I sat down by my lamp and began to draw."

"Now that's what I wanted to hear," said the notary happily.

The girl got up and laid a large sheet of drawing paper on the desk. It read: "O honored Father, after a long and fruitful life, may you find peace and rest in the earth," just as she had lettered it the night before.

"So you remembered," he said gleefully. But when he read it through once more—it was meant to adorn his own tombstone—he had another thought. "Hmm . . . Why not 'peace and rest in heaven'?"

"But that's not the way you dictated it to me," said the girl uneasily.

"Of course, of course. But the inscription on one's own grave is very important. I want the sort of inscription that will enable someone a hundred years from now to understand who I was by reading it."

"I once read a very nice inscription in the Jewish cemetery: 'Ashes to ashes . . .'"

"That's a Jewish inscription," said the notary with a defensive gesture. "Don't you realize that Christianity has lifted man to the level of the Son of God? And if there is no crucifixion and no resurrection, then everything we do here is vanity of vanities. . . . Wait a minute! I just thought of something. Take this down, quickly!" And as soon as she was ready, he began to dictate, "I have extinguished my light . . . and returned to dust, the better to shine in heaven. . . ."

When she stopped typing, he asked, "What are your plans for this evening?"

"Well, first I have to go to the dressmaker's. You see, I'm

having a new blouse made, an art nouveau print with wide
red stripes on white silk and buttons all the way up to the neck.
Very Miss Goody-Goody. The kind governesses used to wear.
The kind Paula Wessely wore in *Masquerade in Vienna* or—if
you saw it—when she starred with Joachim Gottschalk in *I'll
Be Waiting.*"

"And what will you do then?"

"Then I'll play a game of tennis, and then I think I'll take
another swim in the river. And this time I may just swim nude
the way the three students did yesterday. And if anyone
happens to be walking along the other side of the river, all
they'll see is a white lady's bathing suit because my arms and
legs are tanned enough to blend with the shadows of the oak
grove." She glanced up at the notary and fluttered her eyelashes, but seeing he had no pity, she added like a good little
girl, "And when I get home, I'll letter the inscription about
how you have extinguished your light and returned to
dust. . . ." But she soon perked up again; she was unable to
extinguish the light of her youth.

The notary yawned, and though his mouth was still slightly
open, his false teeth had already clapped shut.

"Thank you," he said, and sat down at his desk. "And now,
before my clients start coming in, let us continue working on
the conclusion of my last will and testament." He leafed
through a sheaf of documents he had taken from a drawer.

Then he stood up and began to pace up and down the
office.

Stopping at the open window, he gazed out over the geraniums and the ridge-tiled roofs down to the river, where the
trees were walking on their hands, and dictated, "My coffin
shall be made of metal and be richly ornamented with a deli-
cate Egyptian design inside and out. The bells . . . *all* the
bells are to ring during the funeral service. The mourning

chamber is to be fully carpeted in black, and decorated with a single magnificent crucifix surrounded by seraphim . . . You mean you're going to go swimming tonight in the nude?"

"That's right. For heaven's sake, what difference does it make? It'll be dark, won't it?" she said, her nimble fingers pounding away at the keys.

"That will be lovely," said the old man. And when he finally noticed that the typewriter had fallen silent, he started up again. ". . . a magnificent crucifix surrounded by seraphim . . . thirty-six nine-ounce wax candles . . ." But hearing the sound of dragging feet outside in the courtyard, he leaned out over the geraniums. An old retired coachman was shuffling across the courtyard. His strange gait made him look as if he were riding a bicycle or skiing. He found a sunny spot, took out his pipe and a special gadget he had rigged up to keep the pipe from falling out of his toothless mouth, cleared his throat, and sat down against the wall, looking for all the world like a withered shrub. But as a young man, recalled the notary, he had worried two wives to death. Whenever the first one wouldn't give in to him, he would pull her by the hair to a big steamer trunk, open the lid, and slam it shut on her long hair and lock it. And the second one—he would tie her braids into a knot, take the picture of Jesus down off the big spike in the wall, and hang her on the spike by the braids so he could do whatever it was he happened to feel like doing. Maybe they enjoyed it, maybe that's the way they got their kicks. Some women really are instruments of the devil.

"Thirty-six nine-ounce wax candles . . ." said his secretary.

"Oh yes! Let's see . . ." He turned around, feasted his eyes for a while on the girl's curly, negroid hair, and continued. "Music is to be provided by the cathedral men's choir. . . . The burial service will be officiated over by three priests and four acolytes, who will then direct the procession to the monument. . . . The procession will be headed by the mortuary director followed by a guard of honor . . . an illuminated cross . . . fifteen horse-drawn carriages . . . and two hearses surrounded by men carrying lanterns . . ."

The typist typed along so fast she seemed to be pouring the metal letters of the testament into a tin can.

A sudden holler from the courtyard next door made the notary lean out onto the window sill.

It was the janitor standing by the open cesspool hollering, Láďa, Lááááááďaaaa."

Finally a window on the ground floor opened and a head of slicked-down hair leaned out and said, "What's the matter, Papa?"

"What's the matter!" the janitor yelled back. "You get out here this minute and give me a hand with this pole. It's due to go down to the river for a rinsing." And he pointed to the rod he used for poking around in the cesspool.

"But, Papa, I just got cleaned up."

"You just get out here and give me a hand, do you hear?" yelled the janitor as he pulled the rod out into the courtyard. A young man in a white shirt ran out of the house and grabbed the clean end. "No, you don't," yelled the janitor. "That end's mine. You take this one."

"But I've got on a clean shirt and a new tie," said the young man in his own defense, "and no one in town has a tie anything like it."

"I *order* you, and I'm your father, and you do what I say. You don't expect *me* to carry the shit end, do you?"

"But what about my new tie? . . . Okay, I'll go take it off." And he turned back toward the house.

"Oh no, you don't! You're going to obey me and obey me right now. For the last time, will you carry it or won't you?"

The young man thought it over for a while and said, "I won't. No, I won't. On account of the tie."

"That's the new generation for you," the janitor roared

up to heaven. "A bunch of pretty boys. And me, your father, am I going to have to take the shit end for the rest of my life?"

"Papa," answered the son, "anyone can tell you that when a guy's about to go out on a date he's not going to want to poke around in the cesspool. How could I even shake Olina's hand?"

"Haven't we forgotten something?" asked the secretary. "The number of death notices you wish to have sent."

"Death notices?" asked the notary, startled. "Put down four hundred. And I want a requiem sung in the Church of St. Giles. . . . Do you have that? . . . Good. . . . The male choir will sing *Animas fidelium,* and after mass the three priests accompanied by the choir will perform the *Libera* at the tomb." As he dictated, he could not help tiptoeing over to the window. He peeped out just in time to see the landlord and his son walking out the gate, taking the rod down to the river to be cleaned off. He looked at the janitor's hands, noted he was carrying the undesirable end, nodded, and went on. ". . . a catafalque decorated in a manner befitting the funeral . . . the front ten pews shrouded in black . . ."

An urgent whistle wailed suddenly out of the brewery courtyard.

The little girl in the straw hat was blowing her new whistle for all she was worth. She whistled and whistled and whistled from under her straw hat until her grandmother ran out of the laundry room, drying her hands on her wet apron, then waving them frantically in the sun.

"What is it now, you little gangsters? Why aren't you playing?"

Rubbing her shoe vigorously on the grass, the little girl whined, "Gramma, Baby Zdeněk did number two all over the rug, and I stepped in it!" And she started blowing her whistle again.

Her grandmother gave her a slap that sent the whistle sailing out of her mouth. "Why, you little bitch! Is that all? You mean you whistled for a silly thing like that? I still have to go to work this afternoon, and you bother me on account of that? When am I ever going to get the washing done?"

The notary shrugged his shoulders and moved away from the window.

"The inscription you did for me yesterday," he said, sitting down at his desk, "the inscription for the tombstone, let's enclose it with the testament. After all, one never knows the day or hour. And when you bring me the new one tomorrow—the 'I have returned to dust' one—we'll just switch them, all right?"

"Very good," said the girl. She enjoyed watching how the old man's false teeth slammed shut before he finished what he was saying. She had also noticed that whenever he was about to sneeze he would make a quick grab for his handkerchief and then press it firmly up against his mouth. She wondered how it would look if the notary had his false teeth on the same sort of black silk thread her grandfather used to have on his pince-nez. Grandfather had had another thread too, one that was attached to his hat on the one end and his lapel on the other, and it was supposed to keep his hat from blowing away. What would happen if the notary sneezed and his teeth were left hanging on a black silk thread like Grandfather's pince-nez or Grandfather's hat?

"Brrr," shivered the girl.

"Are you cold?" asked the notary.

"No, just goose bumps. Someone must have stepped on my grave." And she put her arms around herself and rubbed her shoulders.

"A beautiful way of putting it," said the notary, and began perusing a commercial contract that had already been stamped, carefully typewritten, bound with a red and white thread, and sealed with a bright red seal. After reading the document through, he stood up and looked out through the open window at the river. He saw the young man's white shirt leaning over the edge of the water and heard the rod swishing around. The janitor's blue shirt blended with the blue of the river. When the two of them straightened up again, they stood quietly looking out over the water. The river reflected the white shirt as brilliantly as the sun, and showed the young man hanging upside down by his feet in the water like a trapeze artist.

All at once the notary whirled around and said, "Get this down! Quickly, before I forget! 'My coffin is my cradle and the inscription on my monument my birth certificate.' Would you read that back to me now, please?"

II

The Schieslers, a farming couple, were the day's first clients. The notary had known them for a quarter of a century, ever since they had first come to him as newlyweds, both carrying prayer books and wearing peasant dress (Mr. Schiesler in riding breeches, top boots, and a hunting cap), both as dignified as royalty. Now they were old and run down and wore normal city clothes.

"And what news do you bring us today?" asked the notary after seating them.

"Oh, nothing much. Except a neighbor of ours just went crazy," said the farmer.

"Well, well," said the notary with artificial surprise.

"It's like this. He had a sow, and she had a litter, and then all but one of them kicked the bucket. So they bottle-fed the one that was left, and it ran after them like a puppy. But when it got big, they decided to slaughter it. And because the pig hadn't ever been registered, the old man went down to the cellar at night to do it, the pig behind him. Like I said, it always ran after him like a puppy. And once they were down there, the pig put its head in the old man's lap because the old man always used to scratch its snout. Anyway, to keep it from squealing, he whacked it on the neck with the ax handle, but all he did was knock over the candle, and because he hadn't whacked the pig hard enough, he had to take a knife to it, and lay on top of the beast a whole hour until it finally bled to death in the dark. Now the pig must have figured somebody else had hit him, so right up until it died it kept trying to snuggle up to him. And when he came up from the cellar, he collapsed on his bed and cried, and there wasn't anything anybody could do for him. So they came and took him away. Palling around with animals—phooey!"

"My God," exclaimed the notary. "Don't tell me you were there!"

"Oh no, his sister gave me all the details. You know who I mean, the one whose daughter has been bedridden for thirty years."

"The one who lives in number 17?"

"That's the one. Did you ever hear how it happened?"

"No, never."

"Well, it all started one day when she went to town to a Chaplin movie, the one with the angel in it. She decided she'd make the same angel costume for her daughter for Christmas. She made the wings out of real feathers. Real pretty it was too. But the little girl caught cold, and that led to brain fever, and she hasn't gotten out of bed since."

"Oh, I remember now," said the notary. "The other brother has a farm at number 26, doesn't he? How are they getting on, Mrs. Schiesler?"

"Oh, fine, just fine. Just added seven acres to their land," she said, her enormous hands resting in her lap. "Of course, their little boy died, you know. Just about a month now since the funeral. Another case of getting too palsy-walsy with animals. You see, they had a colt that learned how to go into the parlor and beg for sugar. But last year during the sugar beet harvest it went into the kitchen, and something must have frightened it because it bumped up against the stove, reared up, and smashed the furniture to smithereens. The old man jumped after the colt, but before he could throw a blanket over its eyes it gave the boy a good kick. Well, the boy's leg began to give him trouble, so they had to take him to the hospital, and while they were cutting off his leg, he upped and died on them. The old man and his wife asked to see their son in his coffin, but the second they got it open they slammed it shut again, because the sawed-off leg was laying right alongside the little corpse. Otherwise, our village is as boring as can be—nothing worth talking about. You don't know how much better off you are in the city. Except—you know where the Král farm is?" The question seemed to brighten her up a bit.

"Number 14?" asked the notary with a smile.

"Right. Well, that stupid old Král went up to the loft with his servant girl, and they went at it with so much gusto that he got a cramp and couldn't pry himself loose from the girl."

"You don't say!" said the notary, looking over uneasily at the typist's blushing, lowered face.

"Oh yes!" said the farmer's wife, tugging at her little red, falcon-feathered hat. "We had to bring over rope and ladders and roll them into a tarpaulin and lower them into the barnyard. God forgive me, but it looked like—we were all carrying lanterns—it looked like that altarpiece . . . you know, Jesus being lowered from the cross. And when we unrolled the tarpaulin his old woman, the one who always made such a big thing about having her daughter raised in a convent, she whipped them so hard the old man passed out. And you know what? The whipping did no good at all. And neither did pouring cold water over them or poking him with a knife.

Finally we had to call the doctor. He clung to her like a convert to his faith."

"A fine kettle of fish," grumbled the notary. "But you can't get away from it. People in the country are much closer to nature."

"That's about all you can say for them though," said the farmer, tugging at his yellow scarf and straightening his green bow tie. "Our religion teacher was nearly raped a while back. You never can tell what people will get a yen for. One day she's walking along the edge of the woods in broad daylight, along what they call Cock's Walk, when a guy in a blue jacket passes her on his bike. Well, she turns into the woods, and all of a sudden up jumps this guy out of the underbrush and says, 'How 'bout a tumble in the grass?' and tries to rape her. But she was in fine shape, our religion teacher, so she kicked him in the balls and made him carry the bike, and kept on kicking him all the way to the police station. It turns out he was a cattle dealer in from Přelouč, and his excuse was he was only taking a leak, but right there in front of the constable, our religion teacher hauled off and slapped him one, and he broke down and confessed to everything and swore he would never do it again. Apart from that, life in the country isn't at all what it used to be." And he gave the notary a knowing wink.

"But, Ludvík," said Mrs. Schiesler, blowing her nose in her batiste handkerchief, but getting it all over her fingers in the process, "why don't you tell about the time you caught the local idiot . . . you know . . ."

"Are you sure it won't be too wild?" asked the notary, looking over at his typist, whose profile was gleaming with pearls of sweat.

"Wild? Not in the least," answered the farmer's wife. "Just another side of life, that's all."

"Not even worth bringing up, if you ask me," said the farmer, almost angry. "Just a lot of kid stuff. You see, I'm on the town council, so when the man next door half poisoned himself on home-brew plum brandy, they called me in for advice. Well, I told them to hang him by the legs from a ladder so it would all run out of him, but it turns out he had already digested the stuff. Then I remembered what we used to do at home with Grandpa. So we buried him up to his neck in warm cow manure, because by that time he was pretty near stone cold. And no sooner had we put down our pitchforks than I heard a strange-sounding bleating from a goat on the other side of the fence. Now what could that be? we wondered. So we climbed the fence and what do you think we found but the local idiot, the one that stutters, right in the middle of . . ."

The notary stood up, put his finger over his purple lips, and leaned over until his ear was in front of the farmer's mouth.

The farmer whispered a few words, and the notary collapsed back into his chair.

"Well, and then we got together some clubs and whips," he continued loudly, "and did we give it to the stuttering idiot. Got rid of his stuttering, though. But what fun is life on the farm? No theaters. No movie houses. No hotels. Nothing."

"That may be so," said the notary, noticing that the paper his typist was holding was fluttering to the beating of her maiden heart, "but, for Christians like us, God is everywhere— on the farm, in the city. Wherever man may choose to reside, God resides there with him, in his heart. All the rest, as you know so well yourselves, is vanity of vanities. And just as we Christians, the Sons of God, enter into a covenant with God concerning our spiritual state, so do we enter into civil covenants concerning our real estate. That is why you have come to me today. You wish to determine what is to become of your property in the case of your demise. Am I correct?"

By this time the country clients seemed to have calmed down a bit. "Right," they answered together.

"Very well then," said the notary, getting up from his chair. "Let us discuss the various forms a testament can take." And while he spoke, he looked out the window toward the other side of the river, where the sun had almost forced the normal colors to evaporate. Suddenly a red and yellow striped boat that looked like an ice cream wagon came into view. It belonged to Mr. Břichňáč, a retired railroad engineer, and both the bow and the oars were adorned with the ornately lettered address of the owner, who was rowing along in a sweat suit, which bore his entire address embroidered in capitals just above the waist, and gym shoes, each of which also sported carefully lettered addresses. The notary feasted his eyes on the river, never pausing in his oration on last wills and testaments, and as the red boat threw red reflections over the water and trees, he thought back to the time many years ago when the whole town had come out to greet the suffragan bishop from Litoměřice. The station had been filled with pretty little girls and baldachins and banners and councilmen and members of the local band, but the bishop's parlor car was delayed, so the stationmaster hurried a freight car on through, and as Mr. Břichňáč—he was the engineer—as he passed the home signal, he leaned out of the locomotive and blessed the platform with an expansive full-arm cross, and the girls immediately began to toss their flowers and the band played "A Thousand Times Do We Greet Thee" . . . all just for Mr. Břichňáč's coal car. Suddenly the red boat disappeared behind the weeping willow, taking with it all its reflections and all its inscriptions. ". . . which is why property may serve as a gauge of the love parents bear their children, who will continue to farm the land they inherit."

The office was suddenly quiet.

"Well, it's like this, sir," said the farmer, wetting his lips. "We were thinking, like . . . what I mean is . . . you see, we want our oldest son Ludvík to get everything, as long as he gives Anežka—that's our daughter—as long as he gives Anežka fifty thousand. Then we could leave it all in his hands now and . . . well, retire." By the time he had finished, he was practically whispering. He was so embarrassed that he stared down at the ground, his chin entirely hiding his green bow tie. "What do you say?" he asked his wife.

"What I'd like you to write in there is for my son Ludvík to hitch up the carriage once a month and take me over to the cemetery." The tear running down her cheek dissolved enough of her cheap powder to form a kind of gruel in and around the wrinkles of her mouth.

"Very well," said the notary. "The young lady will take care of checking the property assessment records. And next Friday I want you to return with two witnesses. Now let's write out a first draft. . . . Take this down, please. . . ."

The notary stepped over to the window, looked out at the river, and thought about Mr. Břichňáč's evening constitutional on his special health-model Premier bicycle, which could be mounted only by jumping off a specially made block onto specially preadjusted pedals and which sported the ornately lettered address of the house where he lived and in which everything was painted, labeled, and numbered, where green and white arrows led you to the garden, black and white to the woodshed, and brown and blue to the toilet. . . .

"Are you ready? All right, now. . . . Should the Lord God summon us to eternity, we leave the following instructions: Primo . . ." And as he dictated, he looked out over the fluid surface of the river.

III

After the midday meal the notary took his walking stick and went out for a stroll. On his way from the mill to the bridge he was passed by two men on a tandem bicycle. They came so close that the handlebars brushed up against his sleeve. The men were brothers—they sold cigarettes and newspapers near the theater—and had gone out for a ride during their lunch hour. One of them was blind and sat in the back; the one who could see sat in front. In the days when the notary still smoked, he had always bought his cigars from them. He enjoyed watching the blind brother make his way around the shop; he liked seeing his smile of recognition the minute he cleared his throat. "And how is the notary today?" the blind man would ask, and turn and reach into the cubbyhole where the notary's favorite brand of Puerto Rican cigar was kept. He could recognize coins by their size just as he recognized the notary by his cough. And now here they were, pedaling along the river, with their reflection following suit, upside down, in the water. For a while their heads disappeared under the skirts of the branches of some linden trees, but their legs kept going like a coupled engine, and the original plus the reflection in the river added up to a fantastic four-wheeled contraption. As he watched them, the notary wondered what would happen if one night they got drunk and each took the other's seat—the blind brother up front and the sighted brother in the back. How far would they get? If they didn't meet anyone on the way, they might even make it all the way home. Maybe the blind brother knew the way home as well as he knew the coins in his hand or the coughs of his friends. And thinking these thoughts, the notary skirted the old, abandoned stables with the red horses' heads on them and came out into the allotment gardens. Then he noiselessly passed by the other cigar store, the one he was always afraid to look into. But out of the corner of his eye he caught a glimpse of the tobacconist's hands resting on a table near the window. They were the hands of a war invalid who had been severely burned by a flamethrower and had received a medal for valor and a cigar store.

On his way down the stone steps leading to the river, the notary surveyed the city with epicurean delight. First he sought out his own colored windows across the river, and then watched a woman in a red jacket carry her wash basket to the river, kneel down and lean over to stare at her face in the water, fixing stray wisps of her hair. At the same time he saw the identical washerwoman lean out of the water, just like the queen of hearts. But then she took a white bedspread out of her basket, leaned down, and splashed the reflection out of existence.

Also across the water, the local vicar was taking a stroll along the embankment. In the river below, the very same priest, dressed likewise in black coat and derby, was strolling along upside down, and when the long black overcoat came up to the red jacket, like a black exclamation mark over a red point, the entire scene took shape in the water too, but—as before—in reverse, so that when the washerwoman smiled her greetings to the priest and he in turn bowed low and doffed his derby, the reflection in the water made him look as though he was scooping the water up in his hat . . . Observing everything that had gone on across the river, the notary squatted down, scooped up some water with his hand, and ceremoniously splashed it over his face. Then he climbed back up the embankment and followed the fences out of the city.

Near the cherry orchard he came across a young woman in a bathing suit who was sitting on an overturned raft knitting a yellow sweater. A naked little boy, lying on his belly on the bridge, was trying hard to fish something out of the water with a twig. The notary sighed blissfully and looked across the river to where the rolling meadows began and a sun-tanned youth— barefoot and shirtless—had emerged on a white horse and ridden into the shallow water. Another horse suddenly appeared, and it was as if the two horses were standing on each other's hoofs. Then the first horse pulled at the reins and dropped its neck and drank from the mouth of the second.

"Mommy, Mommy, what's this?" asked the little boy, holding up a limp object in front of the young woman in the bathing suit.

"Throw it away right this minute!" she said, blushing.

"But what's it for, Mommy?"

"Throw it away, do you hear?"

"Not till you tell me what it's for!"

"You've got plenty of time left to find out. Now throw it away!"

"But I want to know," whined the little boy, stamping his feet. "I want to know."

"And I want you to throw it away," she yelled, putting aside her knitting. "Understand?"

But the little boy ran away, and his mother started out after him. When she stretched out her hand to catch him, he responded in desperation by stuffing the object he had fished out of the river into his mouth.

"Wait till I tell Daddy on you," yelled the young woman, and began spanking the child, who then tripped and fell at the notary's feet.

"A fine mess," said the notary.

With one hand the young mother tried to pull the object out of the boy's mouth; with the other she went on spanking him, yelling, "You just wait till I tell Daddy, you little brat!" Finally she tore the object out of his mouth and with a great display of disgust hurled it as far away as she could.

Not long after she had gone back to her knitting, she suddenly got the feeling she was riding along on a bicycle and someone had stuck a stick between the spokes of one of the wheels. She turned around and saw the old man undressing her with his eyes. He dwelled on her body with such expertise and such titillation that she instinctively covered her lap with one arm and her breasts with the other. She walked backward in that position until she reached the raft, then picked up her knitting and held it in front of her.

"Hm . . ." grumbled the notary and, pulling his hat down over his eyes, he started back, twirling his cane between his fingers and childishly flipping the blossoms off the flowers with it. He watched the horse swim around with the youth on its back, and as it began to emerge and climb up out of the river, he watched the upside-down horse gradually materialize in the water beneath it. For a while the two horses pawed at one another, but when the rider gave the horse a good solid kick in the belly with his bare heel, it splashed off through the shallow water, obliterating its reflected image.

By this time the notary was in somewhat of a hurry.

Passing the cigar store, he again made a point of not looking in, but once he had passed it, he realized he had not even caught those red hands out of the corner of his eye. He stopped when he heard someone moaning, went back, and peered into the store. There on the floor lay the invalid in an epileptic fit. He was stretched out between the shelves and the chair, buried in a pile of cigarettes.

The notary went around to the entrance but found the door locked. Then he went back to the window and saw the key sticking in the lock from the inside. He put down his cane, raised the sliding window, and twisted the upper half of his body into the tiny store. Straining to reach the key in the lock, he lost his balance and fell head over heels inside. The first thing he noticed as he started to fall was the red hands scarred by the flamethrower. When he finally came to rest, he found himself lying with his face on top of the invalid's, a face so damaged by the war that it looked as if it had been immersed in boiling oil. The notary's heel pulled open the drawer of a small desk, and a few handfuls of coins showered over them.

Then, finally managing to free one hand, he unlocked the door and tumbled out into the sunshine.

At just this point the woman who sold the evening daily rode by on her bicycle, her papers piled high on both front and back carriers. When she saw the notary somersaulting out the door and the invalid lying inside among the coins and cigarettes, she jumped off her bike and froze—her legs straddling the crossbar, with her hands resting on the handlebars.

"Give me a hand with him, Mrs. Vorlíčková," said the notary.

But the newspaper vendor was frozen to the spot. The notary dragged the tobacconist—and the cigarettes and coins—out by himself. Then he unbuttoned his shirt, slapped his face a few times, and wiped away the saliva. By this time the newspaper vendor had pulled out of it, and though she still seemed unable to put anything in motion but her thumb, she at least began ringing her bicycle bell.

People came running. They pried open the invalid's clenched fists and brought water from the river to sprinkle over the poor fellow's chest. The notary sat stroking the man's head in his lap. After the treatment it had gotten in the war, it looked like a rag doll made of different kinds of leather.

"Go call his wife, Mrs. Vorlíčková, would you?" said the notary to the newspaper vendor. At this, she added a wail to her bell ringing.

"Pick up the money and the cigarettes, everybody," said the notary, continuing to stroke the tobacconist, and he looked out across the river and saw a fisherman baiting his hook with a tiny, live fish, lively and shiny as a mirror. Careful not to harm its backbone, he threw it in a wide arc into the water. There was another fisherman sitting opposite him in the river's mirror like the king of spades.

"And run get the doctor," suggested the notary.

AT THE SIGN OF THE GREENTREE

Ever since streetcar No. 13 missed the turn out in front, crashed through the window, and plowed on as far as the tap, the Greentree had failed to attract the clientele it once had. Not that this bothered Mr. Chlumecký, the tavernkeeper, any too much. What he still looked forward to most in life was the first beer he drew for himself when he got up in the morning. Today that morning beer had been only the first of a steady stream. Standing by the glass door, he read and reread a death notice that ran: "I hereby advise all my acquaintances that I, Julie Kadavá, secondary school teacher, have died at the age of 67. My funeral will take place at the Ďáblice Cemetery on September 16, 1961" (the date was written in pencil). It was signed, in the hand of the deceased: "Julie Kadavá, secondary school teacher."

Every time he read it Mr. Chlumecký would shake his head, go back to the tap, rest both hands on it, draw himself a beer, down it all at once, and then slosh the glass around in the sink.

It was growing dark, but he had not turned on the lights yet. His only two customers were sitting up against the back wall next to the cellar door—just in case the No. 13 should stage a repeat performance.

"How many steps does Pasovský's Tavern have?" asked one.

"Seven," answered the other. "What about Kalenda's?"

"Kalenda's? Which one? There's the one over by the academy or the one down on the embankment."

"God, don't you know anything? The academy Kalenda's was closed down long ago. The Kalenda's opposite the private pier is the only one left."

"Wait a second. One . . . two . . . three . . . four . . . five," counted the man, stepping down the stairs in his mind. "Seven in all, and they go down. What about the Good Source?"

"One up. And the Red Hearts?" And so on. The bartender went back to the door in time to see a No. 14, lit up like a night club, heading straight toward him at full speed, lighting the whole place up too, and then at the very last moment jerking to the side at what was nearly a right angle and running parallel to the Greentree with only a narrow passageway separating it from the front window. Its cars looked like three illuminated aquariums.

Along came Chlumecký's brother-in-law. "What brings you to this neck of the woods?" he asked, opening the door. He was clearly delighted to see him.

"Well, why don't you ever come visit us, you old son of a gun? Mařka can't even remember what you look like."

"When I come," said Chlumecký, drawing a beer, "I'll come in style. I'm going to buy a motor bike."

"You?" asked his brother-in-law, giving him a whack in the stomach. "With that pot of yours?"

"That's right," said the bartender, drawing himself a beer, drinking it down in a single gulp, and sloshing the glass around in the sink. "I've got to do something for my body. I'm nothing but a shadow."

"Of the fat man in the circus," said his brother-in-law. "But really, František. Don't get a motor bike. The accidents I've seen! I was driving the No. 13 one day, and what should I see out the window but a madman just like you lying next to his motor bike. Before the wheels could stop turning they had covered his face with the morning paper and the cops were drawing a circle around him. What an unholy mess! No, don't even think about a motor bike. Really, don't. Listen to what your old brother-in-law tells you. Don't get a motor bike."

"But it's hardly bigger than a regular bike."

"It's little farts like that can get in the worst crackups. Once we wedged this fat lady on a motor bike between a No. 14 and a No. 13, shopping bag and all. Those trolley cars were like a vise. And all I did was wait there with my brakes on. I wasn't going to go look, not for anything in the world. That last little yelp was enough for me. All I did was stand behind the second car and smoke and wait for the commission to come. We were on a pretty steep upgrade, and when I looked down I saw a stream of milk and fresh blood running down the tracks."

"So you think I ought to get a car instead," said Chlumecký, irritated. He went over to the door and began drumming his fingers on the glass. The No. 10 almost scraped the green paint off the wall but then changed its mind and turned, wallpapering the whole joint with its yellow light. Right on its tail came a No. 12. The conductor of the No. 10 stood on the back platform of the last car and drew a question mark in the air with her finger, and the driver of the No. 12 held up three fingers, sadly, meaning he had three more rounds to go before the tram went to the garage. The conductor nodded sadly back, showing that she sympathized with him. Then she gave him a big smile, held up only one finger, closed her eyes blissfully, and drew a long dash in the air, meaning how happy the thought of only one more trip made her.

All this time Chlumecký's brother-in-law had been carrying on with his stories. "I could go on like this till midnight. A car is just as dangerous—four wheels or no four wheels. Once a Morris Minor got wedged in between a No. 5 and a No. 19. It was like crumpling up a newspaper. There were these two women in the car, see? And the one who was driving decided to try to spurt ahead. But she didn't make it. Why, they were wedged in so tight it took grappling hooks to get them out. One piece went into the first coffin, the other into the second. In the end there were more or less two women again, I guess. But I say forget it."

"Then the only thing left is to walk."

"Walking's not so bad, just you make sure you don't walk around with your head in the clouds," said the bartender's brother-in-law, shaking his head. "František, you wouldn't believe the way people throw themselves under streetcars. And on the straightaway, too. Why, there are people who stand there on the curb looking both ways, and as soon as they see a streetcar coming, they seem to say to themselves, 'That's my baby!' and run right under it. Once I had an inspector, he was after one of those ticket collectors, and he crawled right under my No. 9. It's not so bad when they die right on the spot, but when the guy under the wheels is still alive, do you have problems. Move up a little, move back a little—all you do is squnch him more. And there he is, screaming, 'Have mercy on me, somebody! Get this weight off me, please!' No, even a walk around Prague's no joke."

"What's a ticket collector?" asked Chlumecký, downing another beer. He went over to the door, looked out, and drummed his fingers on the death notice in which the deceased advised her friends of her death and invited them to attend her funeral.

"You only find them in Prague, and they're mostly on pension. They collect used streetcar tickets that still have time left, and then they take free rides with them. It's a great sport. I know one hospital director who gets a huge charge out of it."

"Hm," responded Chlumecký. "Say," he said, turning to his only two customers, "have we been disturbing you?" But they were shouting so loud they didn't hear him. It was an argument about how many steps led up to the Hinterland.

"Why don't you pack up and go have a look for yourselves?" said Chlumecký.

"Good idea," said one of them, putting on his cap. And out they went, hands in their pockets, in the direction of the tram stop.

"Four steps," said Chlumecký's brother-in-law.

"I'd only take the motor bike out on picnics and things like that, you know," said Chlumecký. "Sometimes I get pretty short of breath."

"I know the problem all right. Your sister Mařka has it too. You can never wait to pack up and rush off somewhere. No wonder every time I stop off at the Hop Bush for a beer I hear the hospital orderlies talking shop, saying: 'Used to be, you know, the only victims of the Christmas season were carps, and the Easter season, lambs. This last Christmas we saw seventeen motorists laid out, to say nothing of missing arms and legs.' They've even got a new department for drivers in the hospital. 'The Garage,' they call it. Once, when I was still behind the controls, I was turning a No. 11 around at the last stop . . ."

"Hold it a second! What do you mean '*still* behind the controls'? I didn't know you'd quit."

"Oh yes. No more for me."

"How come?"

"Well, it was all because of this woman . . ."

"You and a woman?"

"Me and a woman. You see, every once in a while on the No. 6 route I would slow down when I got to the last stop and watch the streetcar guiding itself around the loop, through the trees, and along the fence and back. Then I figured out an improvement—and this was where I broke the rules. I would put it on automatic and drop into the Terminus Tavern for a quick coffee. And just as I finished and came out into the open, the trolley would come around the bend all by itself and I'd jump aboard and brake her."

"But what about the woman?"

"Oh, her. She was a peroxide-blond conductor who was going to driver's school and kept begging me, 'Mr. Konopásek, please let me take her around the loop by myself.' And because she wore her lipstick the way I like it, I finally gave in. So from that time on I would finish my coffee and wait for her to stick her little red mouth through the door and say, 'Here I am, Mr. Konopásek.' One day I waited and waited, and finally I went to have a look. It's pitch-black out, so I walk around the loop and back to the straight stretch of track in front of the Terminus, and my heart stops cold. No tram. What can I do, I say to myself, but walk to Strossmeier Square and find out what's what? Let me tell you, I've never seen Prague as beautiful as it was that morning. I found my conductor friend sitting on the second step of Maršíček's Tavern, her head in her lap, and the tears running down her face like there's no tomorrow. 'What's the matter, Zdenka?' I ask her. And she gets down on her knees and clasps her hands together and begs, 'Forgive me, Mr. Konopásek, forgive me.' And in a flash I realize what has gone wrong. 'Zdenka, you were on your way around the loop when the wheel trolley came undone, right? And you forgot to put on the brakes before you went out to hook it up again, so it started up without you.' 'Yes, and you should have seen it jump when the power came on,' she said. 'What did you have the controls set on?' I asked her. 'Full speed ahead.' And when I heard that I put my head down in my lap too."

"Ah, women," said the bartender.

"So anyway, I walk to the Strossmeier Square, and on the way I have this vision of a colossal wreck. But when I get there the square is empty. Then the track switcher calls me over and looks out at me like an owl from his little booth and says,

'Konopásek, Konopásek, where's the No. 6? Do you have any idea what you've done? With the chief streetcar inspector sitting here beside me, what do I see but an empty car go shooting across the intersection, breaking every rule in the book. "I must be out of my mind," goes the inspector. So he pinches himself in the arm and on the cheek and then jumps up and says, "No, I must really have seen it!" and runs out onto the street. Lucky for you, he found some taxis at the taxi stand by the Rustic Pub. Anyway, they didn't catch up with the streetcar until the King of the Railroads, and it wasn't until the bridge that the inspector finally managed to jump aboard—a real Harry Piel jump it was, too—and bring it to a halt. It's a good thing the 11 or the 18 or the 8 or the 2 weren't late crossing the intersection. Man, what a wreck that would have been!' "

"You know what?" said Chlumecký to his brother-in-law. "I don't think I'll buy that motor bike after all. . . . Anyway, what did they do to you?"

"Pretty near cut my balls off," grinned Konopásek.

Chlumecký drew himself another beer and said to the empty room, "Hey, guys, you know what? Let's get drunk!" And when he'd downed it, he sloshed the glass around in the sink and shook his head. "I certainly won't get that motor bike now. It might run in the family. Though I wasn't scared in the least," he added, holding onto the tap, "when the No. 13 crashed through up to the tap here. When the dust finally settled, the first thing I did was turn to the driver—who was still at the controls—and say to him, 'Friend,' I said, 'how do you want it? Light or dark?' But now I'm plenty scared. No, sir, no motor bike for me."

"But why shouldn't you buy a motor bike if you think you'd enjoy it? What could be nicer than an outing in the country? Some fresh air in the old lungs?"

"Well, I was just thinking about all those awful pictures of accidents you see in police stations and insurance offices—awful! And I'd have to cut down on my drinking too. No early morning beers."

"Come on, František. What harm can a little beer do? In fact, a glass of beer is just the thing to give you the confidence you need to get around those blind curves. Of course people have accidents. But there's no law saying you have to be one of them. Go ahead and buy one if you feel like it."

"You really think so?"

"Go ahead. You've got a driver's license, buy yourself a motorcycle if you want. Then we can go out to the country and pick apricots. Or apples."

"Yes, but what happens if the chain breaks or the back wheel gets stuck? What then? I'll be flat on my back before I know it."

"Look, František. Without a little luck you're not even safe going to take a leak. You can break a leg in your own home, you know. But say we do have an accident. We won't be the first, we won't be the last. You've got to take some chances. What would become of us if we never put anything on the line?"

"You're absolutely right," said Chlumecký. "I *will* buy a motorcycle. But in the meantime you know what I look forward to most? Getting drunk again when I'm sober. On beer."

"Here, let me turn on the lights," said Konopásek, getting up.

"No, don't. Not yet. People would start coming in with pitchers for beer," he mumbled into his glass. Then he smacked his lips and sloshed the glass around in the water.

The two men who had gone off before came back. They sat down at their table without a word.

"What did you find out?" asked Chlumecký.

"Four steps up," said one of them.

"Well, I'll be going," said Chlumecký's brother-in-law. "The old lady sent me out to buy her a record of the theme music from that *Moulin Rouge* movie, and I have an old um-pah-pah waltz picked out for myself. Women sure give you a hard time. It used to be she'd give her right arm for a brass band, but they're my favorite too, so she's switched over to jazz. When we first got married, we both rooted for Sparta. By the time six months were up, she crossed over and turned into a Slavia fan. If Sparta wins against Slavia by a big enough score, she won't even talk to me. František, buy yourself a 150-cc. machine. You can always sell it and pick up something more powerful. The faster it is the better you can work your way out of a tight spot. That fat woman, remember? The one we crunched between the 3 and the 14? Well, if she'd been on a 250-cc. instead of a motor bike, chances are she would have shot right through."

"Really?" asked Chlumecký.

"How many steps is it up to the Pelc Tyrolka?" asked one of the men at the table.

"None," said Chlumecký's brother-in-law saucily as he went out the door. "You enter at street level."

Another streetcar was on its way down, and Chlumecký once again stood protectively over the tap; he had caught sight of the clearly lit 13 on the front of the car. And just like all the other streetcars coming down the hill, this one looked as if it was going to crash into the front window. The tavernkeeper let go of the tap and ran over to the cellar door, put his foot in the doorway so he'd have a head start just in case the 13 came barreling in the way it had the other time. . . . But all it did was veer and light up the whole room.

Mr. Chlumecký drew himself a beer, and when he had downed it, he said to himself, "Good beer they have here. I'll have to stop by more often."

Then he walked over to the door and switched on the lights.

DIAMOND EYE

The passenger had already placed his foot on the first rung of the railroad car steps when he felt somebody tugging at his arm. He turned around to see a middle-aged man standing on the platform.

"Excuse me, but are you going all the way to Prague?" he asked.

"Why, yes, I am," said the passenger.

"Then you wouldn't mind taking my daughter Vendulka with you? She'll be met at the station in Prague." He delivered a girl of about sixteen into the passenger's hands.

The stationmaster blew his whistle, and the conductor first helped the girl into the car, then signaled with his hand that the train was ready to go. The stationmaster gave the final signal, and the train was off.

The girl's father ran alongside the train yelling, "Vendulka, we've got our fingers crossed. And as soon as you know, send us a telegram! Can you hear me?"

"I hear you," she called to him. "You want me to send a telegram."

When the train had passed the ALL CLEAR AHEAD signal, the passenger opened the door and led the girl into the corridor. He was still holding her by the hand and had no idea what to do with her.

"Really!" began a monologue issuing from a nearby compartment. "Once, even before we were married, she went to buy me a shirt, but she couldn't buy anything, because she didn't know my size. She was nearly out the door when she had an idea. 'When I go to choke him, I always have my hands like this.' So the salesman took a tape measure and measured the circumference of her hands and said, 'Sixteen.' And see? The shirt fits like a glove. . . ."

The doors slid open, and out ran a bald-headed man doubled up with laughter. "No, he's just too much!" he cried, banging his fist on the wooden wall of the railroad car.

Once he had calmed down a bit, he went back into the compartment, where the same voice continued its story. "So I said to myself, if she could go out and get me that shirt, well then, I'll surprise her with a little hat for Christmas. So I go to the high-fashion *modes robes* and I say, 'I'd like that pretty little number over there in the window.' And *modes robes* says to me, she says, 'What size would you like?' Well, at first I didn't know, but then I had an idea. 'Once, when we were having a quarrel, I gave my fiancée a little love tap like this. She had the feel of her head in my hand ever since and from that day to this I have the feel of her head in me.' And *modes robes* brought me out hat after hat, and I tried each one of them under my palm until finally I yelled out, 'This is it!' And I put it under the tree, and it fit her like a bedpan fits a fanny."

Again the bald-headed man burst out of the compartment, pressing his handkerchief to his mouth, gasping for breath. He pushed the girl aside, stuck his head out the window, and again began beating his fist against the wall. "He's too much, that guy. Too much!" he said, wiping away his tears.

The passenger who had been entrusted with the girl—he was still holding her hand—followed the bald man resolutely into the compartment.

"Gentlemen," said the girl when she had gotten inside, "my name is Vendulka Kříštová and I am going to Prague!" She stretched out her hands and felt her way in front of her. The first thing she touched was the curly head of the storyteller. "My name is Emil Krása," he said in response.

"And I'm Václav Kohoutek," said the bald man.

The man leading the girl brushed up against the bald man's head while putting his briefcase in the luggage rack overhead.

"Can't you watch what you're doing, damn it?"

"Sorry."

"Did somebody hit somebody?" asked the girl. "That happens to me all the time. I'm the one who takes our letters to the mailbox and I knew the way there and back like I know my own name. Then one day those damn mailmen switched it two buildings closer, and I rammed my forehead right smack dab into the corner of it and hurt myself. But I got even. All it took was a few whacks of the old white stick."

"Come sit over here by the window," said the bald man, wiping his eyes. "It'll give you a better view of the scenery."

The girl first felt around for the seat and then for the window. She held out her hand parallel to the ground, as if she were testing to see if it was raining. "How nicely the sun is shining," she said.

The passengers fell silent.

"Was that your father there at the station?" asked the man who had taken her from him.

"Yes, it was." She nodded. "What a character he is, though! Everyone is jealous of me. My father grows fruit for a living, and once he ran over our crippled neighbor with his delivery truck. And there was a trial, and all Papa's enemies were as happy as could be. 'Serves him right,' they said. 'Now he'll either get thrown in the clink or have some steep fine slapped on him.' But who should come running crutchless into the courtroom, chipper as you please, but our neighbor, the one he'd run over. She couldn't get enough of kissing his hands and thanking him for doing such a good job; she could walk again, without the crutches. 'If only you'd run me over thirty years ago,' she said, 'I might have found a husband.'"

"Sounds like a fine father you've got there," said the curly-headed man.

"Don't I though," she said, laughing. She put out her hand again, but just at that moment the train went into a curve and moved the sun from the compartment window to the corridor window.

"Sun's gone down," she said.

The passengers looked at one another and nodded.

"What does *your* father do?" she asked, placing her hand on the knee of the curly-headed storyteller.

"He's been in retirement for the past fifteen years because he's got the biggest heart in all Europe. His heart is as big as a bucket, and it sits right in the middle of his chest."

"Sure, sure," said the bald-headed man.

"Why, that's wonderful," cried Vendulka.

"I'll say," continued the curly-headed man. "Father has a contract with the university: when he dies, they get his heart. Some foreigners once offered him quite a pile, but he's a real patriot. He wouldn't give it to them for anything. Father's not allowed to go swimming or fly in an airplane or even ride an express train."

"I know why!" cried the girl. "So his heart doesn't burst or get lost. Right?" She felt around for the hand of the curly-headed storyteller and squeezed it. "Fathers like yours and mine are one of a kind!"

"That's right," he said with what looked very much like a blush. "Sometimes I go to the university with him. First they take all his clothes off and then they draw blue and red lines all over him."

"Right! Right!" said Vendulka enthusiastically. "Because the red lines are arteries and the blue lines veins!"

"Right," said the man, covering her hand with his own.

"And then they take him into a big room and the students crowd all around him and bend over him and the professor points all over him like he was a map, and explains things. And then he hooks up a student's heart to a megaphone, and it sounds just like a toy drum or a soldier marching up and down the hall of a barracks. Then, when they hook up my father's heart . . ."

"It's like a thunderstorm in the distance!" cried the girl. "Like a splitting boulder! Like tons of potatoes pouring down into the cellar! Like Emil Gilels playing the piano!"

"Exactly," said the curly-headed man, surprised, and he loosened his collar.

"You can't imagine how happy I am to be here with you!" she exclaimed. "How nice it is to know that someone else has a famous father too!"

The train was running parallel to a paved road. It passed a billboard picturing a big blue heart with two streams pouring out of it. The text read: FOR YOUR HEART TRY THE WATERS AT PODĚBRADY SPA.

A feeling of mystery pervaded the compartment.

"The professor at the university just can't wait to dig into that strange heart with his scalpel."

"Of course he can't," said the girl. "And now another Czech heart will become famous."

"But who can measure up to *your* father?" said the bald man, taking down his briefcase.

"Oh, absolutely," she said. "But you have to see my father to believe him. You ought to watch him dance," she cried, clapping her hands. "When we roll up the rug there's always a circle around us. Papa does a great solo too. Once, when he slipped the bandmaster a bill and was about to launch into his favorite song, a policeman came along and told him he couldn't sing. Well, one thing led to another until pow! Papa slammed him one on the nose. I should have told you right off: the policeman had a crooked nose to begin with. Oh my, the blood! And then Papa did his singing act. Well, all the neighbors were as happy as could be. 'Old man Křišta's gone and done it this time!' they said to one another. But when the trial came up four months later, the handsome policeman swore he had asked for, even ordered the punch in the nose. He had nothing for Papa but the most heartfelt thanks. You see, before Papa hit him, his nose had been bent over to the right. And Papa's punch straightened it out so nicely that the daughter of a rich farmer fell in love with him and they got married. Instead of thank-you notes they send Papa a platter of cakes and cookies every summer, and in the winter some fresh pork every time they slaughter."

"Now who would have thought that a punch in the nose could lay the basis for a happy family?" reflected the bald passenger, putting on his coat.

"What does your papa do?" asked Vendulka.

"He has gone on to a better world," he said. "He was such a good father that it's taken me until now—now that he's gone—to realize it. He always worked the night shift, and when Mama would hear the gate creaking in the morning she'd fill the tub with boiling water. Then Papa would leave his allotment in the courtyard . . ."

"Allotment of what?" she asked.

"The coal that miners brought home in a huge pocket sewn into their coats. Then he'd come upstairs and take off his clothes. Mama had already put on the coffeepot, and he'd wash up and sit and eat his bread and wash it down with coffee. And while he ate and drank he would take off his boots and put on his good shoes and get dressed up. He always managed to finish his coffee and put on his cap at the same time. And then he'd go off to the Blue Star for cards with the boys, and at lunchtime I'd take him his lunch, and he'd eat it while he played. At four he'd come home and lie down on the floor—to give the old skeleton a chance to straighten itself out, as he used to say. And when he'd had his sleep he'd go back to the mines. But one day Mama filled the tub . . ."

The train had begun to slow down, and the bald man gave Vendulka his hand. "Best of luck. This is where I get off," he said on his way out into the corridor.

The train came to a stop.

Vendulka felt along the window for the handle, pulled it down, and called out onto the platform of the country station, "Mister! Mister! Tell me how it ends! Tell me how it turns out!"

The bald man stepped up to the window and went on. "Mama filled the tub with boiling water, but Papa didn't come home. When the water had cooled off she went out to look for him. In the doorway she stumbled over Papa's pipe . . ."

The train started moving, but the bald man trotted alongside to keep up. "And Mama picked up the pipe and burst into tears. She wrapped her shawl around her and ran over to the mines. . . . Papa had been crushed to death by a rock. . . . His friends had come to tell her. . . . But they just couldn't do it. . . . So they put the pipe up against the door and ran away. . . . You know, I never saw my mother asleep? . . . She was always up by the time I got up. . . . When I went to bed . . . she was always mending something. . . . It wasn't until later . . . that I saw her asleep. . . ." Finally he stopped and took a deep breath.

"Please forgive me, sir. Sir, please forgive me for having a father who is still alive! Forgive me, sir. Forgive me!" Vendulka cried out.

After a short silence the man who had been entrusted with the girl said, "My father was a tanner, and he had a disease they used to call old man's blight. Year after year they had to cut off more and more of his legs until in the end he went around on a little cart. He planted roses for a hobby. They covered the whole wall of the tannery. They were called tea roses and they were yellow. Papa knew exactly how many there were. He was the only one allowed to cut them, and he would only cut them for the church and for young ladies. Then one day they built a street through our wall, and that was the end of the tea roses. Father thought it would be the end of him too until he thought up another hobby. He'd ride out to a very dangerous curve in the road and direct traffic. First with his hands and later with a flag. From morning to night, even in the rain. I had to wire an umbrella to his cart. He kept it up for eight years, and when he died there were hundreds of trucks at his funeral, and the curve where he had stood was covered with flowers. This high!"

"How high?" asked Vendulka.

"This high," he said, lifting the girl's hand to the proper level. "But when they started having accidents there again, they put up two large mirrors."

"My, oh, my, you have a famous father too," she said. "A father who changed into a mirror. Into two mirrors!"

The passengers first looked at one another and then out the window. The train was just coming into a town with two round mirrors, like a gigantic pince-nez, reflecting a blind curve.

A feeling of mystery pervaded the compartment.

The passenger escorting the girl cleared his throat and said, "Your father looked quite thin there at the station."

"You should have seen him a year ago. Round as a butterball. With cardiomyoliposis and all sorts of liver, stomach, and kidney trouble thrown in. Mama said it came from a disorderly way of life. The doctor put him on a diet, but Papa was weak-willed; he liked to eat. Then one day the herb woman advised him that the only thing that would help him develop his will power was to go say something very insulting to the police. Well, it worked! They took him down to the station, and Papa dictated his insults into the records and signed his name to them, and they gave him six months. And were his enemies overjoyed! 'Thank God, that bastard will be out of our hair for a while,' they said. But when Papa got out he was as skinny as a rail, and the first thing he did was hold a press conference at the Garland, treated everyone to beers, and said, 'Let me tell you. There's no diet anywhere that's as efficient as jail. And not only am I hale and hearty; I picked up two thousand crowns to boot.' And he showed everybody how big his coat was on him, and all our beer-bellied neighbors had to admit there was no one quite like old man Křišta. . . . You know what would be nice if you don't have anything against it? Why not come to one of our Thursday evening dances? We could trip the light fantastic!"

"Dance?" asked the curly-headed man, slightly taken aback.

"Why not? I'm grown up enough, aren't I? But let's hold off for another two months, okay? The doctor told me that when I got to be sixteen he'd operate on me, and my operation's set for this week! Then I'll have a chance to see this beautiful world too. I'll see people and things and the countryside and my work. I'm sure those baskets I weave are beautiful! I'm sure the whole world is beautiful!"

"You are?" asked the man she had boarded the train with, forcing a smile.

"Oh, and how! It's just got to be!" she cried. "There's a man who works with me who had an unhappy love affair before he came to us. He was so unhappy he kept scratching around under his eyelids with an indelible pencil. Finally the doctor said to him, 'Look here,' he said. 'If you do that once more, you won't see any more of this great big beautiful world.' And the man said, 'I'm through with this great big beautiful world!' And he went back to scratching around under his eyelids with an indelible pencil. Now he's weaving baskets with me, and does he howl about how he misses the world. . . . The world must be beautiful, as beautiful as your father, who changed into two mirrors. Oh, in two months I'll be able to see! Will you do me the honor and come dance with me?"

The door slid open.

"Tickets, please," said the young conductor, yawning with boredom.

A PRAGUE NATIVITY

When the locust trees growing in the synagogue courtyard
bloom during the summer, they look like falling snow. It had
been snowing heavily since morning. Over by the fence a
woman was hammering away at an orange crate and stacking
the boards in a baby carriage. On the other side of the synagogue there had once been a graveyard for sets and props,
things even amateur actors had left behind: a plaster Venus covered with dirty drawings, stairs leading up to nowhere, a broken
mirror, sofa springs, and excelsior. The rain and snow had
taken their toll, and the lowest layer had begun its trip back to
the earth, turning into a humus speckled with rusty nails and
glass. Here and there something that, given a little imagination, actually looked like something stuck up out of the pile.
When the stagehands went outside to take a leak, they would
first guess, then argue, and finally present evidence to prove
that one piece of junk was a branch from the Forest of Arden,
another the headboard of a bed from *The Merry Wives of
Windsor*. And since the neighborhood boys had broken nearly
all the windows with their slingshots, the locust branches
grew right into the synagogue, and old props peeped out.

But the most beautiful time of year was just before Christmas. Every year, then as now, people came here to buy their
Christmas trees. They would choose one from what looked like
an actual grove of pines and firs and then knock it against the

123

ground to untangle its branches and give it a chance to show whether it was perfect all by itself or needed an extra branch or two to fill it out. Today it had been snowing since morning, and the courtyard was fragrant with pine needles.

The stage manager began his discourse even before they got to the synagogue. "Man's finest trait, Milton, is a good memory. And when it doesn't function the way it should, you have to use a picture or a memo book together with a tape measure."

"I agree," said Milton. "It's just that I'm afraid Mother Nature never meant for me to use a tape measure. I always seem to have my head in the clouds."

"You don't say."

"Oh yes. On my way home I don't breathe easy until I'm sure there's no fire engine on our street and my place hasn't burned down. It's only when I walk up the stairs and there's no torrent streaming down them that I know I didn't forget to turn off the water. But I can't relax completely until I'm sure the radio hasn't caught fire and there's no smell of gas."

"Well, I have a terrific memory. And when it fails me I write everything down. What is a memo book for, anyway?"

"That's all well and good, but I'd keep losing my memo book."

"Tell me anything, Milton, anything but that. I'm sure your memory is every bit as good as mine. You're just pulling my leg. Now give me the keys."

"What keys?"

"The ones I gave you yesterday. The ones to the little church."

"I don't have them."

"Milton, hand over those keys."

"But I gave them back to you yesterday."

"You did? Then they must be back at the theater."

"In your locker."

"Okay then, wait here. But don't go anyplace. I don't want to have to start looking for you."

"Say, aren't those the keys in your pocket?"

"Well, so they are!" he exclaimed happily, reaching into his pocket. He stepped up and unlocked a tall iron door on which a combination of rust and fungus had painted pictures of turbulent storm clouds.

The door opened, and some greenish plaster drizzled down from the roof. As the two men stepped inside, they could see their breath in front of them. They ran up the winding staircase to the balcony, where furniture from plays no longer in the repertory was kept. The dust made it all seem majestic and mysterious.

"Today we're going to get the inventory over with. Watch where I write everything down."

"Why?" asked Milton a bit nervously.

"Why? What if I should die? Or fall ill? . . . You see? There's a picture for every piece of furniture. Isn't it beautiful?"

"If you say so," said Milton, bringing over a sewing machine.

"That's from *The Day They Stole Prague*. By the way, who ever thought up such a nice name for you, Milton?"

"My mother," said Milton, pointing down to his belt with his chin. "When my mother was carrying me around in here, she picked up a book called *Paradise Lost* and decided if it was a boy his name would be Milton. The sewing machine is No. 22."

"Check. Here's its picture. And here—in case something should happen to me—here is where you tick it off in red. Did you ever read the book?"

"No."

"What a pity. Maybe your mother lost some kind of paradise."

"She probably did—when she had me. No, I'm not much of a reader."

"Pity. Say, what did you do before you got into the theater?"

"I sorted medicinal herbs."

"And you gave it up?"

"I started getting the odors mixed up. I got overodored."

"And that's why you gave it up?"

"That was part of it. But partly because I was always a season behind. When linden trees were in bloom they'd bring me dried celandine and bird cherry. And it wasn't until the mulleins had begun to bloom that they brought me linden blossoms. Everything a season late. . . . You know where they put the inventory number on this table? On one of the legs!"

"Impossible!" cried the stage manager, jumping out of his seat.

"Have a look for yourself."

"Well what do you know! *The Star without a Name*," said the stage manager angrily, and checked off the table with his red pencil after showing Milton the picture in his memo book. "Cold in here, isn't it?" he said, walking over to the broken window. He stuck his hands out and warmed them in the snowstorm.

"You do have a good memory," said Milton in admiration.

"Just a matter of practice. When you've been in the theater as long as I have, you'll be able to pick up any piece of junk and tell right off where, when, and in what it was used. I don't want to flatter you or anything, Milton, but you ought to try and work up a little more feeling for the furniture. All it would take is a little effort. Aren't you interested in getting ahead?"

"I've always been like this. A season behind in everything. Long after the guys started brushing their hair the new way, I still greased mine down and parted it in the middle. They would wear tight pants and fitted jackets, and I'd still go around with my trouser legs flapping and my shoulders padded. They'd be out on their motorcycles, and I'd still be taking walks through the fields and picking bluebonnets like an idiot. They were all married long ago, and I didn't fall in love and get married until very recently."

"So you're married?"

"Uh-huh. This iron chair is No. 220."

The Houses of Mr. Sartorius. But let's forget about that for a while, and come over and warm your hands. It really is warmer out there. Is she a good wife?"

"She's a stray angel. Her parents used to have lots of money. Their old house is a church now. Truda and I once went out there to have a look around. It was Sunday. People were going up the steps. And inside, in the house she'd once lived in, there was an organ playing and people singing 'Draw Near to Thy Savior.' Truda stood up against the white fence, smiled, and whispered to me, 'Only five of us used to live here, and now look how many people there are.' It's great, it's really great."

"Really?"

"Really and truly. Once we took a trip to the mountains, to where her parents used to have a summer house. We stood at the fence there too. And thirty little kids came toddling out the door, and their teacher sat down in front of them and read them a fairy tale. And Truda said to me, she said, 'How wonderful. Only five of us used to live here, and now there are thirty children. Milton, how much richer I am now than I was before. A church where people have a chance to sing and a nursery school where children hear fairy tales—it all makes me feel so good inside, Milton.' How about let's getting on with the work?"

"Wait a second. I'm glad to see you're starting to take to the furniture, but let me first tell you something about my house. Twenty-five years ago I made up my mind to build myself a temporary house on a piece of land I had. So I went to let the authorities in on it, and when I told them, one of the officials said, 'You're not building any house on that land. There's going to be a highway cutting straight through it.' So I said

127

to him, 'And if I go ahead?' And he said to me, 'You'll go to jail.' 'For how long?' I asked. 'Six months,' he answered. Well, I gave it a little thought, put on my hat, and said, 'You've got yourself a deal!' And that fellow followed me out yelling, 'Then we'll tear it down.'" The stage manager's voice carried out the synagogue window and down to where people were buying their Christmas trees. Some of them looked up, but they could not see in the window because the snow was falling so thickly.

"What does your wife do?" asked the stage manager after savoring fully the memory of the past as if it were a new present.

"She's a window dresser. Now she's always a season *ahead* of herself. When people are all bundled up in winter clothes, Truda is decking her windows with green twigs and golden suns and dressing her mannequins in spring outfits. And when people are wading through the spring slush, my wife is filling her windows with bathing suits and things, crowned with a 'Where will you spend your vacation this year?' sign. And by the time Truda and I get around to swimming in the Vltava, she is ready to order her colored foliage and start dressing her wax dummies in duffel coats and tweed suits."

"Milton! You must have read that somewhere!"

"No, really. Look, I tell you what. Tomorrow you can go take a look for yourself. You'll find her in the show window at Čapek's. She'll be wearing sweat pants, a fur jacket, ski boots, and one of those Russian hats. And her cheeks will be bright red from the cold. But what she's putting on display is nylon underwear and evening gowns. Because Truda is living in January and February. She once told me that when she was a little girl and all the other little girls were playing with their dolls she would dream about her first boy friend. And by the time that first boy friend came along she was thinking about having children. Always a season ahead of herself—that's my wife. Crazy, isn't it?"

"Milton, let's get back to the furniture. But just so you have some idea of who you're dealing with, let me finish my story. My house was all built, and I was just putting the finishing touches on the fence when who should drop by but my friend from the land office. 'I've come to inform you that we are going to tear down your house.' Now I'd heard him only too well, but I thought I'd give him a chance to change his mind, so I asked, 'What was that you said?' And when he'd repeated what he'd said about tearing the house down I picked up an ax and bellowed, 'Just say that one more time!' Well, he started backing off with his hands out in front of him and his eyes on that ax, and me yelling, 'Just what did you mean by that?' Soon one hand began feeling around in back of him for the latch in the gate, and finally he said, 'That we're not going to tear your house down.' Then he opened the gate and disappeared." And arms akimbo, legs spread wide, the stage manager proclaimed from his balcony, "That house is standing to this day."

"You were perfectly right. After all, you built the house yourself," said Milton, taking down a large wicker basket.

"I should say so. And if anybody tried to take it away from me I'd trample them all underfoot."

"Oh, I'm sure you would. . . . Man, is this basket heavy!" said Milton, guiding it onto a trunk with his knee.

"Sir John Falstaff. *The Merry Wives.*"

"No. 106."

"Let me write it down. . . . That's right, and here's the picture. . . . Milton, there's something I want to tell you. Just wait till you hear this. We've decided to put you in charge of furniture! All this belongs to you. You'll have the key to everything," said the stage manager gleefully, and with a sweep of the hand he took in all the treasures covered with silken dust.

"That's wonderful news," said Milton, "but what if it all went up in flames on me?"

"I feel the same way, every time I come in here, but don't worry. You won't set a match to it. You're extraordinarily conscientious. In fact, everyone in the theater has to be at least a little out of the ordinary. What kind of showman can you be if you don't jump out of bed at night? Haven't you ever noticed that the worst catastrophes in the world are caused by nice people?"

"I'm not so sure. . . ."

"Well, let me tell you, it's true. You know, we must have done something awfully wrong: the inventory shows we have everything we should. By the way, have you seen my red pencil anywhere?" And he went over to the window to warm his hands in the December blizzard.

Mr. Bedar's favorite expression was "We're all here by the grace of the gravedigger." Mr. Bedar was a sorter of medicinal herbs, and every morning just after six he stopped in at the Portrait of the Virgin Tavern and drank up the five crowns his wife had given him for lunch. Then he went from table to table hawking his midafternoon snack, and the money thus earned went straight into bitter-smelling brandy. And when that was all gone he said happily, "And now if I climb a tree I'll have no reason to come down. You ask me why? Because," he answered immediately, "we're all here by the grace of the gravedigger." After which he set off for work.

As he sat there sorting camomile from plantain, all he thought about was whom he could touch for a loan. The people he worked with refused to lend him anything any more, and his credit at the bars in the area was so bad that for his midafternoon break he was forced to take the tram to a place where he was unknown and could order a drink, toss it down, and then make some sort of deal about putting it on a tab. "He's a real character, a welfare case," his boss used to say, in an attempt to justify himself as much as his employee. And Mr. Bedar would get back at his boss whenever he saw him getting ready for a snort at the counter by pulling his friends' sleeves, pointing at his superior, and whispering, "Looks like the cash box will be short again today!"

One day Mr. Bedar decided to take the tram to visit his friend Milton who used to sort herbs with him. He got off at the theater and walked past it until he came to the first tavern.

The manager, on his way out of the kitchen with several orders of sausage, stopped in front of the kitchen side of the thickly padded door and yelled, "Go ahead. Lap it up at my expense. You bunch of beggars . . ." Then he gave the door a shove with his knee and waltzed into the restaurant.

"Enjoy your meal," he said to the men after handing each his sausages. And the two men, who the day before had lit the first fire under a boiler they had repaired and decided that, since the boiler had finally wet its whistle, they would follow suit, took the manager's words as a good omen, ordered two shots for themselves, and added, "One for that guy over there too."

"Right away, right away," he said, enunciating each syllable with great care, but back in the kitchen, when the sound of their singing began to penetrate the closed door he cried out, "Scream your lungs out for all I care. But why am I always the one to pay? And treating a total stranger to boot." And he spat on the floor and gestured at the door with his fist. Then he took out his wallet, found the slip of paper that showed how much they owed him, and waved it violently in the direction of the door, bellowing, "That makes seven crowns, and no end in sight. Who do you think's going to pay, anyway?" His eyes were bulging as he waved the bill at the closed door. Then he smoothed down his wrinkles, waltzed into the restaurant with a smile on his face and, after listening a while to the singing, remarked, "What fine voices they have."

A mailman, who had been sitting over by the stove, in a fur coat and hat, replied, "Like unmilked cows." And pointing to the blue mail wagon, he added, "You know, we won't be having any of those much longer. The post office has stopped accepting packages over thirty-five pounds."

"That's nothing new," put in Mr. Bedar, clinking glasses at a distance with the boilermakers. "You're all going to be replaced by women."

"Right," said the mailman, closing his eyes.

"What are you mailmen going to do once they sell your horses?"

"We haven't the slightest idea."

"Well, I'll tell you. They'll put a woman up on the driver's seat and two mailmen will take the place of one horse."

"Whoa, there! Not on your life," said the mailman, and spat on the floor.

"Well then, what *do* you want to do?" asked Mr. Bedar, all ears.

"Something dignified," answered the mailman.

"Well, I've heard rumors that the mailmen who get the sack are going to have to go around picking up garbage at the railroad stations or shooting sparrows in the parks."

"I've heard that too," interrupted the manager. "But tell me: is it true that a mailman has to have a gun on him when he's delivering money?"

"That's crazy."

"Wait a minute," said the manager, dismissing the mailman with a wave of the hand. "I was told at the main post office that, if a mailman is carrying money and somebody attacks him, then he's supposed to shoot himself so the robbers won't get him alive. That's why he's got to have a pistol on him. Isn't that so?"

"Absolutely," answered Mr. Bedar. "In fact, there's even been talk of having mailmen perform the public service of delivering drunks to their doorsteps. But only at Christmastime, of course."

"Are you trying to put something over on me? Why, I'd be the first to know!" said the mailman, pointing at himself.

"Ha! Well, let me tell you what I heard from one of my highest superiors! Starting next year, as soon as I have a drunk on my hands, all I have to do is hang a tag around his neck, write his name and address on it, and our mailman will be obliged to take him home."

"Who do you think you're talking to?" said the mailman, getting up from his chair.

"Sit down, sit down, Pop," said Mr. Bedar, trying to soothe him. "You've got no choice in the matter because you're under oath. Of course, only if they sign for him."

"Well, if they sign for him . . ." said the mailman, calming down.

And the manager brushed all the crumbs off the tablecloth into the mailman's lap and sighed, "Oh, those poor, poor mailmen. Why, there are some parts of Prague where, when people don't pick up their shoes from the shoemaker's in time, the postmaster calls in his men and says, 'Take these bags of shoes and deliver them with the mail C.O.D.'"

"We don't know where our next meal is coming from, and now this!"

"Well, what do you want, anyway? You think they'll let you spend all your time guzzling beer?" asked the manager, astonished.

"You Prague mailmen have it easy as it is," said Mr. Bedar. "Why, in the country, when they're not delivering the mail, they're out feeding stray dogs. And don't think the Society for the Prevention of Cruelty to Animals has anything to do with it. No, sir. That's the way the people want it. Then if somebody has trouble getting hold of a mailman, all he has to do is look out into the street for a pack of dogs, and the mailman is bound to be close by."

"Oh no, not that. Anything but that," said the manager. "If we had that system in Prague, how would I ever keep the dogs away from the tavern? If I were postmaster, I would decree that in winter mailmen be allowed to bring their horses at least as far as the hallway. It isn't fair to leave a faithful beast out in the cold." And to show how far the horses would be allowed to go, he stretched out his arm and knocked over the mailman's beer.

"You did that on purpose!" cried the mailman angrily, jumping up and stamping to get the crumbs out of his lap.

"Why don't you take off your clothes and let them dry?"

"No, there's no point. Not for such a short time."

"Sure, sure. You've only been here two hours now." The manager glanced out the window and scowled. Through the window he spied a bunch of gypsy children drawing airplanes and rocket ships in the snowdrifts along the wall opposite the restaurant. "The minute I see them I have a fit. It's awful. Where do they get it from? When they've drawn as high as they can reach, they just pull up a chair and start in again where they left off. And in summer? They draw all over the pavement in front of the reTaurant. And don't think they let up when it gets dark. No, sir. They're down on all fours, crawling under the street lamp and drawing, drawing, drawing."

"But they're only kids," said a coal heaver who had been sitting in the corner. "You ought to see the old men, the ones on pension. If it gets dark in the middle of a game of cards, they move the whole table over to the street lamp to keep it going. Or if it's checkers they're playing, they put the board on the wall under the lamp and never miss a move." What they first noticed when he got up was the leather apron on his back and his soot-circled eyes. He stood there for a while looking down at his hands and finally said, "When I think that in the past thirty years I've loaded so much coal in my scuttle that if I put all those cellar stairs end to end I could climb clear up to the moon." But right away he thought better of it. "No, not to the moon. But even with my scuttle on my back I could take a nice walk along a rainbow. Could I have my check, please?"

"Me too," said the postman.

On his way out the coal heaver gave the manager such a hearty handshake that his wedding ring ground a little niche into his finger. But that didn't keep him from laughing and bowing—until he had run back into the kitchen, taken a look at his finger, given his hand a good shake, and yelled "Watch out there! You're getting a little too fresh for my taste!" into the door. Then back he went into the taproom, closing the door behind him with an elegant flip of the ankle. At this point the front door opened and in walked Milton the stagehand, numb from the cold.

"Welcome, Milton, welcome!" Mr. Bedar called, holding out his hands to him. "Gentlemen, this is my friend Milton. We used to work together."

"Mm . . ." sighed the stagehand.

Mr. Bedar patted him a few times and then fingered his coat sleeve. "What a beautiful jacket. English cloth. They don't make them like that any more." Then, slapping him on the back and feeling his shoulders, Mr. Bedar announced triumphantly, "A punch from him and you think you've been kicked by a horse. Do your duty, Milton. Take up wrestling. Why, with your double Nelson you could put anybody's shoulder out of commission. Even *I* couldn't fight my way out of it. And those legs! I've never seen the likes of them. Milton, why not at least play some soccer? You'd have it all over the forwards they give us nowadays! Here, let me treat. Waiter, two brandies. And put them on my tab. You know, Milton, I was talking with the higher-ups the other day, and guess what I said when they asked me who was the best worker we ever had?"

"I have no idea," whispered Milton.

"Well then, I'll tell you. I said *you* were, Milton. You!" And then, as if something outside had caught his eye, he leaned up against the window sill and began to observe the snow falling. After a while he sat back in his chair and asked, "Well, how do I look?"

"Great, just great," answered Milton with a smile and, fixing Mr. Bedar's eyes, he saw those two anxious little fires he could never resist. He reached into his pocket, crumpled up his last ten-crown note, and offered his hand to his friend. Mr. Bedar shook it and slipped the money deftly into his pocket.

"Holidays coming up . . ." he said sheepishly, and drank down first his own drink and then, after asking permission, Milton's as well. "Well, I'll be going now. . . ."

"I'll take care of it," said Milton, pointing to himself.

"Shall I add it to your tab?" asked the waiter.

"Yes, please," nodded Milton.

Mr. Bedar took the waiter's flabby hand and, holding it in his, went into the following exposition. "You run a good place here, and I won't be forgetting it. In every bar people say something nice. At Pinkas' someone crying into his beer once said, 'True education means self-ruination!' —At The Golden Tiger a judge said, 'You can't weave a cat-o'-nine-tails out of manure, and even if you could, you wouldn't be able to crack it.' —The accordion player at Kolčavka's once said, 'A real man always has a slight hangover, a slight cold, and a hint of cow piss about him.' —A student wearing glasses at The Two Grandmas said, 'Modern art is a corn-infested toe whose core is a fungus-infected grain of barley.' —At Rozkošný's a tiny conductor said, 'Inferiority complexes are man's crowning glory.' —At The Golden Palm a man wearing a monocle confessed, 'Anything I say I immediately refute.' —At Tichák's a janitor's wife said, 'Dirty words are prayers to stop dirty deeds.' —A waitress at The White Lamb said, 'How is it I'm so lonely when Prague has so many people?' —At The Angel a milkman prophesied, 'Modern man will begin to walk.' —And a girl at Šenflok's proclaimed, 'One deep experience is worth a whole university library.' Really something, aren't they? And they're being said every day in every bar."

"And what will you take away with you from here?" asked the manager, whose hand was still clasped in Mr. Bedar's.

"I will never forget your coal heaver saying that if he ever stretched out all the stairs he's run down he'd be able to climb with his scuttle to the moon. Well, I'll be off."

And he said good-by with tears in his eyes.

When he had gone, the manager motioned toward the window and said, "Charming fellow, don't you think?"

Raskolnikov rose up out of the audience, laid his hand on his heart, and said, "I have a great deed to perform today." Then he stepped into the courtyard of the house on Gorokhovaya Street where the pawnbroker and moneylender Katerina Ivanovna lived.

Milton was sitting in the wings on Sonya's bed when along came Badouček, another stagehand, and sat down beside him. To keep himself from thinking about something that was bothering him, Badouček began telling Milton a story—in a whisper. "It all started right around this time of year, just before Christmas. I remember it as if it were yesterday. We were doing an autopsy on a suicide. Our regimental doctor washed his hands and then said to me, 'Badouček, here in this sack is Private Fikar's heart. Be careful with it; it's a rare specimen. I want you to deliver it to Professor Jirásek at such and such a hospital.' So I clicked my heels and said, 'Yes, sir!' and off I went. The heart was in a flour sack and was about as big, well

—about as big as the head of a baby. When I got to the hospital I asked at the gate whether I could see Professor Jirásek, and they told me he hadn't come in yet, so I went down to the Black Brewery for a beer."

An electrician, who had just fixed a cockeyed spotlight on the bridge and come down the ladder into the wings, whispered as he passed the bed, "Are you in for it!"

"Don't worry," said Badouček, and went on with his story. "While I was drinking my beer I met a man named Julda, a blond guy with a dent in his forehead, right here. He told me it came from a refrigerator compressor that had blown up and left him so bad off that they decided to give him extreme unction. 'Man, I wake up there in that hospital,' he told me, 'candles all around and heads with wings bending over me. It was a while before I realized they were nuns praying for me. So I said, "Where the hell am I?" and those nuns went for the chief doctor and the chief doctor sent for Professor Jirásek, and the two of them stood over me, and the chief doctor said, "Professor Jirásek, this guy's making a comeback." But Professor Jirásek said, "Nah, he's as moribundus as they come. Just give him whatever his heart desires." So the first thing I did when I woke up from dying was to ask for a bottle of cognac! And when they brought it, I drank it down one, two, three and passed out again. The next morning when I woke up I told them, "I wouldn't mind another bottle," and the day after that I had a third. By which time I was beginning to come around. So Professor Jirásek paid me another call, took a look at my head, and said, "Well, what do you know. It's resorbing. Keep him on cognac." Well, after the thirtieth bottle I stood up. Thanks to the golden hands of Professor Jirásek!' That's what Julda told me. And then I told him, 'Julda, wait till you hear this.' And I told him I was waiting to see Professor Jirásek with the heart of Private Fikar, who shot himself through the head on account of an unhappy love affair. But I never should have

told him, because he kept pestering me to let him see whether
the heart had really broken in two. But I told him, 'Look,
Julda. I'm on official business. I can't show it to you.' 'Well,
the least you can do is let me carry it,' he grumbled, because
he'd already made up his mind to come along with me and
say hello to Professor Jirásek and thank him again for the
golden hands that had shown him the way. So we each drank
three cognacs to Professor Jirásek's health."

By this time Raskolnikov had left the pawnbroker's and was
mumbling to himself, "The first step. That's what people fear
the most. The first step . . . The first step . . ." The stage went
dark, a brown net came down from the rigging loft, the stagehands began running around quietly setting up tables, a kero-
sene lamp glided down on a wire, and the prop man's green
skull emerged from the black velvet backdrop whispering,
"Where is the ax? Has anyone seen an ax around here? Look,
I'm just getting over a heart attack. What am I going to do?"
Then, as suddenly as it had appeared, it slipped back into the
deep purple darkness.

When the stage lights came on again, Titular Councilor
Marmeladov picked up his bottle and said, "Gentlemen, I am a
civil servant."

Badouček clasped his hands under his knees and said, "And
then we had one more for the road, and Julda got going about
how after we got through with the hospital he'd take me to see
his wife. 'She loves me so much,' said Julda, 'that when I bring
someone home she gets all dolled up and runs out for veal cut-
lets and bakes my favorite cake. Hey that hospital isn't going
anywhere, you know. Why not stop and have another drink at
Stromeček's, and if nobody's there, I can take a peek into the
sack.' So we took our time about it. Julda kept putting his ear
up to the bag and shaking it like it was an alarm clock or something. I told him there was no point in it because the heart was
stone cold, but he insisted that the heart must have some

remnant of the girl he killed himself for and that if we cut into it we would certainly find a picture of her. . . ."

"So my daughter took to the streets, and I lay there drunk," said Titular Councilor Marmeladov to Raskolnikov, raising his hand to his heart.

"Milton," said Badouček, clearing his throat, "do you think Jihlava is going to win the game today?"

"Dukla, hands down."

"I've got some money on them," said the stagehand. He was sweating.

"Everyone's got to have a place where he belongs," cried out Titular Councilor Marmeladov.

Stagehand Badouček ran his hand over the back of his head and continued his story. "So we stopped in at Stromeček's and had two cognacs, and when we had finished those the manager came over and asked, 'Two more?' But I jumped up and said, 'No, definitely not. We have to go to the hospital.' And this time we hustled. But when we got there they told us at the gate that Professor Jirásek would be in the operating room for the next two hours. So Julda started spouting off again about how we ought to go home to his place and how his wife would be decorating the tree and would make us some punch and then go out for the meat and bake a cake. . . . Hey, the scene is almost over." Badouček got up.

Raskolnikov was leading off Marmeladov dead drunk. The lighting was pale, almost lurid. Then the stage went dark, and on came the stagehands with boxes and barrels for the courtyard.

During the next scene the eye of the spotlight lit up a part of the courtyard just out of reach of the fire inspector, who was sitting just behind the proscenium arch asleep. He kept leaning over toward the light, which seemed to have some magnetic power over him. It was as though a speck of it on his person would cause him to somersault onto the stage.

"Should I wake him up?" asked Milton.

"Let him have his fall. We could use some fun around here," Badouček said with a wave of his hand. "But that guy," he added, pointing to the prop man, "that guy there will die an unnatural death." By this time he had found his rubber ax and was waiting in the corner to give it to Raskolnikov when the time came. "You know what he did once? In the second act, when he's supposed to give Sonya a lighted candle from behind the screen, well, a minute beforehand he realized he'd forgotten the matches. 'Hey,' he whispered. 'Anyone got any matches?' But nobody did, or if they did, they didn't hand them over—just so they could see what would happen. When Sonya put her hand out he stuck an unlighted candle in it. Sonya shielded the flame with the other hand, because it was in the script, and held it up to the faces of the passers-by so she could see who they were, but there wasn't any flame. And the prop man—by then he was bent over in horror—staggered off whispering to himself, 'What a catastrophe! What a catastrophe! Oh, my heart!' The actors enjoyed themselves no end, of course. So did I. But what about the game in Jihlava?"

"Dukla'll win it cold," said Milton. "Of course a game is a game, and the weather is always an important factor . . ."

"What?"

"The weather. I could hear the trains yesterday. That means a change in the weather."

"Right."

"I set great store by those trains. Why don't I go have a look? Is there still time?"

"Wait," said Badouček, peeking through a hole in the velvet. "Okay. Go ahead. Raskolnikov has just stabbed the old lady and is washing his hands in the bucket. You've got plenty of time."

"Then I'm going," said Milton and, skirting the wings, he felt his way along the wall as far as the gate.

He lifted the latch and the door opened a crack. The sky was pink and the air soft. Across the way a television screen in a dark apartment on the second floor shone like a big blue full moon. From the switching yard on the other side of the hill came a loudspeaker voice intoning, "Track 36 . . ."

Milton closed the gate and went back and sat down on the bed.

Badouček was unable to stand the lull. "So we went to Julda's. There was a woman there fixing up a Christmas tree all right, but as soon as she laid eyes on us, did she let him have it. 'Don't you see you're making me a nervous wreck? Where'd you put the money?' And then she turned to me. 'Look what you've done to him, you filthy swillpot! I'm calling the police!' So I grabbed the heart out of Julda's hands and made a run for it. This time when I got back to the hospital, the man at the gate waved me away. Apparently Professor Jirásek had left and wasn't expected back the rest of the day. Say, how is it out, Milton?"

"You can hear the trains even louder than before."

"Is it raining?"

"Everything but."

"That's good," said the stagehand plaintively.

A backstage hurdy-gurdy struck up a sprightly Italian opera melody.

"Does Jihlava have an indoor stadium?"

"I don't know."

"I'm going to go take a look at the weather for myself," he decided.

He felt his way along the wall, opened the gate, and looked out into the pink-bluish night. It was drizzling and the snow had turned yellow. The synagogue on the other side of the street was as dark as the trunks of maples in early spring. Near the piles of Christmas trees a stray dog named Sylva, a cross between a German shepherd and a St. Bernard, left her doorway shelter and trotted along the sidewalk to the entrance of the synagogue. The snow crunched under her paws. Someone stuck a hand through the door and patted the dog, who then trotted back to her doorway. In the morning, when the first customers made their way to the grocery and meat shops, Sylva would mingle with them, waiting for the leftovers the salesgirls gave her. Her route would take her from shop to shop up to the Cross. There she would take a nap, and in the afternoon make her way down again, arriving at the synagogue toward evening. She had been going on like that for ten years now, and once, when she had an abscess, the people living along the street took her to be operated on by Dr. Wele. Badouček saw her dragging herself through the wet snow, probably on her way to lie down in the doorway and dream about a barrel around her neck and snowed-in mountain climbers.

He closed the gate and went back.

"I bet I'll have a good Christmas," he said, "like the year I brought the heart back to the colonel. 'Professor Jirásek wasn't in,' I told him. 'Here's your heart back.' But no sooner had he taken a look into the sack than he screamed, 'It's completely spoiled, you moron!' So I picked it up, carried it off to the boiler, and threw it into the fire. No, Jihlava doesn't have an indoor stadium. I just remembered. And Dukla's bound to lose in all that mud and slush. There goes my two hundred and thirty crowns."

Sonya Marmeladova, wearing a straw hat with artificial cherries and two yellow braids, curtsied to Raskolnikov and asked him politely, "Will you be coming to the funeral?"

LITTLE EMAN

He still didn't feel quite like going home yet, so he said to himself he ought to stop off for a cup of coffee. It had already begun to grow dark, but he could still make out the figure of old Mrs. Ziková limping along in front of him.

"Beautiful evening, isn't it, ma'am?"

"Get along with you, Eman."

But little Eman kept at her. "Where were you yesterday, eh? I'll bet you were off two-timing me with the chimney sweep."

"And what if I was? He's a good boy."

"A show-off if ever there was one."

"Don't make a scene right here in public, Eman. People know me."

"Aha. Now you're worried about what people will say. Well, I know what would happen if I left you alone one minute with that chimney sweep. I can just see you making eyes at him."

"Eman, people are staring."

"I know your kind. You'd give in right away."

"No, I wouldn't."

"Oh yes, you would. I can tell you get all hot and bothered thinking of the chimney sweep's body."

"And what if I do?" she asked, delighted.

"Well then, I wouldn't take you on the outing I thought up just for the two of us."

"Why, you dirty little pig, you," she said, ecstatic.

"You," whispered little Eman into her gray curls, "you would cling to me like ivy around an arbor."

"Eman! What about the people! I don't want another scandal in my building."

"So what! Let them envy a real woman who still has someone to drink in the magic of her eyes. Ah, what a silky neck you have!"

"Eman, I'll tell your mother! But first tell me more about that outing."

"Well, we'd walk along together, barefoot of course. And then, with your tiny alabaster foot . . ."

"Shut up, for God's sake. Or at least don't shout like that."

"And then we'd have a true Walpurgis Night, a night of love."

"Let me go, you idiot! Let me go, I tell you!"

"All right, all right, but first you've got to hear me out. You know what I dreamed last night?"

"I couldn't care less, but I bet it was something dirty. Remember how the Nazis beat your head in? Didn't that teach you a lesson?"

"The only reason I'm telling you is that I love you so much. You see, the dream I had was about you."

"I don't want to hear another word."

"Not even about the lucky rabbit hutch?"

"No. I'd rather have a pound of pork."

"Or about happiness in a barn?"

"I'd rather have a pound of beef." By now Mrs. Ziková had begun to get annoyed, because she'd just recalled that she had been retired for two years.

"So that's the way it is, you old witch. You wouldn't say no to the chimney sweep, would you now?"

"Maybe, maybe not. But, Eman, why don't you find some young girl to pester with your attentions?"

"But you're not even pushing fifty."

"How old?" asked Mrs. Ziková, happy again.

"Forty-five."

"Sixty-two in January. But let me go. Let go of my hand. I have to go get something to eat. And when I see your mother I'm going to tell her everything you said."

"Just see if she believes you!"

Little Eman knew that Mrs. Ziková would walk along the creek to her home on the outskirts of the city. He gave her his hand and said gravely, "Good night, Mrs. Ziková."

"Good night. And next time you see me, come and walk a ways with me again. You make me feel good inside, you little devil. I'll be laughing all the way into bed."

She shook his hand warmly, and suddenly her eyes were moist. But in no time she was limping her way along the babbling brook.

Little Eman crossed the main street, walked through the cafeteria, and climbed the stairs to the dance hall. Even though it was near the edge of town, the dance hall had a downtown feeling to it. He took a seat on a high bar stool and leaned up against the counter. "The usual, please. Gin and tonic. But what's this I see? Why so sad, Olympie? Why so sad?"

"Oh, you know, Eman . . ." she said with a sigh.

"An affair of the heart?"

"What else? I've lost him, Eman. I've lost my everything. He wants to be alone, he says."

"He wants to be alone? Him? That's a laugh!"

"But that's what he says. 'You've made my life hideous,' he writes. Tell me, am I that ugly?"

"Listen, Olympie, when I look at you . . . how shall I put it? Anyway, I may have found a girl or two behind the bar at The Monika or The Barbara that's in your league, but nowhere

147

have I ever seen anyone with eyes like yours. You always seem so bedazzled."

"There, you see? And I made life hideous for him. But I know what he's getting at. He's quite a character, you know."

"Tell me, what do you mean by 'character'?" asked little Eman, and then immediately answered his own question. "A character is a person who insists on believing what he has made up about himself. Take me, now. I'm no character. I was born in '24. We had to be adaptable. Scene One. We have just dug ourselves out after the raid on Düsseldorf. An asphalt road. The remains of the city in the background. A small child emerges from the debris on roller skates. There is a jug of milk in his hands. Scene Two. The attack on Gleiwitz. Bombs falling. I look out the bunker window. A factory district. The Busch Circus is in town. The cages shoot into the air. A lioness sees how the latch works and opens it with her paw. Eight lions run out into the flaming city. We are turned out and formed into a rescue squad. Flaming streets. Lions. Caesar, the biggest of the lions, grabs a woman who has passed out and runs up the stair to the top floor of a flaming apartment house. There he stands in the window with the woman in his teeth, looking out over flaming Gleiwitz . . ."

Little Eman tapped his forehead. "And I've got thousands of other scenes like that up here. That's why I'm the type that's always changing. I couldn't possibly be a character."

"Well, I'm always the same, Eman. I always have the same problem."

"Him?"

"Him and only him. Have you ever noticed, Eman, how old-fashioned I am?"

"You, Olympie? Why, you could . . ."

"I know I could. Have a guy around every finger, right? But you know, it just wouldn't seem right to me. If only I didn't love my Joska with such an old-fashioned love! Why, I cried a quarter of a pint of tears over that letter."

Little Eman stroked the back of her hand. "Calm down, Olympie."

But the girl was swimming in tears. "All he's waiting for is for me to start going out with somebody else. Then he can write and say, 'Now I see how much your love for me meant to you.' But I'm too smart for him. He's just testing me. I'll hold out. I'll just be a stay-at-home, that's all."

"You, Olympie, a stay-at-home?" asked little Eman. Just as he was about to stroke her hand again, a giant of a man took the seat next to his. Eman recognized him right away, he was Alfréd Bér, the furniture mover.

"May I help you?" asked Olympie.

"Rum!" thundered back a virile voice.

"What's wrong, Mr. Bér?" asked little Eman, watching Olympie fill his glass.

"I'm sick of life," complained Alfréd Bér, putting out his hand. When Olympie put the rum down on the counter, he sheltered the glass like a tiny bird.

"Oh, we all are sometimes, Mr. Bér," said little Eman. "But everyone has something he loves."

"I'm sick of everything, I tell you," said the giant, and he tossed the rum down his gullet and slammed the glass back down on the counter. Then he stared down dully at his hands. They looked like maps of Asian mountains.

"Olympie, just look at those fine hands. What a sight!" said little Eman, and looking into Alfréd Bér's sad eyes, he whispered, "What I wouldn't give for hands like those."

"Aw, what good are they anyway?" said the furniture mover, shaking his head. "No one appreciates them any more."

"What good are they? Well, I could show people how I move the things they love from one place to another. After all, everyone has something he loves. Isn't that so?"

"And what do you love?" asked Alfréd Bér, raising his eyes.

"I love the piano. Oh, I don't play any more; the things I could play I didn't like and the things I like I wasn't good enough to play. So I'd like to have my piano moved over to my sister's place. She's got a little boy, and I figure he can use it. But just between you and me, Alfréd, can I trust my piano to some mover I never even saw before? It's a Georgswalde, you know. Very valuable."

"So it's important to you, is it?" asked Alfréd Bér, smiling and perking up. "You know what? Let me move that piano for you, and with these very hands. But I want you to be there so you can see what they can do! When can I come?"

"Olympie, two rums on me!" ordered little Eman. He thought for a moment and said, "How about tomorrow? I should be back from the mine by four, so make it a quarter past. What do you say?"

"Right you are!" bellowed Alfréd Bér, engulfing little Eman's hand in his own. "Wait till you see how careful I am. Wait till you see these hands and this back carrying your piano out onto the street!"

When they'd finished the drink, Alfréd Bér got down off the stool and said—to himself more than to anyone in particular—"Everyone has something he loves."

"Everyone," said little Eman with a smile as he watched Mr. Bér tread across the dance floor where no one was dancing because the music did not begin until after nine.

"Eman," said Olympie, "Eman, you must really have an education."

"Humph. Never got through grade school."

"What difference does that make? You always get to the bottom of things. And you've got feeling. Joska says that somewhere deep inside you have a little starling on a string. I remember how once, when Joska and I were down by the river, he pulled out a bunch of papers with typing all over them and said to me, 'A friend of mine has written something. Here, let me read it to you.' So I lay down on my back, and he read me story after story."

"Story after story? What kinds?" asked little Eman, and finished off his glass.

"Well, here's one I remember." She breathed into the glass and wiped it off with a napkin. "It was getting on to the end of the war, and the Germans decided to transport a trainload of women away from the concentration camp at Oranienburg. But on the way American fighter bombers shot the locomotive to bits and damaged the rest of the cars too, and all the SS men took off. The women scattered too, and two Jewish women who had been wounded by flying shrapnel hid in a little patch of woods by digging holes for themselves among the fir trees and covering themselves over with branches. Before long they heard the hounds scouring the woods, but somehow they managed to go undetected. Anyway, they lay there right through to the next day, and just when they began feeling sure they would die there, they heard voices speaking Czech. It was our boys from the Nothilfe. They pulled the women out, bandaged them up, and hid them at night under their beds. When the front caught up with them and everybody was making a run for it on their own, one of those Czechs—Pepík, his name was—loaded one of the women onto a cart and carted her as far as Bautzen, where they waited for the front to pass. And then he carted her all the way to Haida."

"Tell me, Olympie! How was it written? Did it sound like it was written about someone, or like the person who wrote it had actually been there?"

"It sounded like the person who was telling it, like it had all happened to him. . . . How stupid I am! Now I see! How come I never thought of it before?" she said, slapping her forehead. "He must have written it himself!"

"Of course he did," said little Eman ironically. "Let me tell you how it ends, okay? From Haida, Pepík took her all the way to Česká Lípa, where the Red Cross took over. And then she waited four whole years for her hero to come claim her, but he never came. So she got married. May I have the check?"

By the end of the story he was no longer looking at Olympie. "What's the matter, Eman? You can tell me. What's the matter?" And she took his hand. But little Eman had the feeling it was only out of sympathy. He was just on the verge of telling her that he, little Eman, was the Pepík in the story, that he was the one who had dragged that Jewish girl all the way from Hoyerswarda to Česká Lípa, that Joska had actually heard the whole thing from him, but when he looked up at her again, he realized that it would only make her more unhappy. So instead he said as cheerfully as he could, "The next time you see Joska, give him my regards, will you?"

Little Eman hurried across the hall and down the stairs to the cafeteria. He ordered something to drink and sat down next to an old woman he had known since he was a child.

"And how's life been treating you?" he asked her.

"Just fine," she answered. "Soup's good today. But hot. Tell me, Eman, do you still work in the mines at Kladno?"

"That's right."

"What's the food like these days?"

"You mean in the canteen?"

"Yes. What sort of menu do they have?"

"Well, on Monday there's soup à la chef, beef stroganoff, and cream puffs with chocolate icing. On Tuesday, collective farm soup and lungs à la viennoise with dumplings."

"Sounds as if they *have* made some improvements. You know, I never had it as good as that. I raised seven children and I still found time to put in a few hours a day as a corpse washer."

"You don't say."

"Oh yes. Not much difference between a baby and a man that's dying. The one and the other are just about as likely to dirty the sheets; it's thinking about what lies ahead that does it. What about Wednesday?"

"Ox tongue à la polonaise. Thursday there's gulash à la Esterházy, and Friday, piping hot coffee and good old Czech buns. But tell me, weren't you ever scared of the corpses?"

"Son, when I was young, there was nothing on this earth could scare me. I've been known to pick up an ax and run out into the dark after robbers. There's one time I did get scared, though. This old, forgotten woman died way off beyond the village in the middle of a freezing cold winter. Well, we get there, see, and put the coffin down on a bench. And the guy I was working with that night, Franta, pulls back the blanket and says, 'Go get me the hammer.' So I go outside—the boss was just riding up on his bike—and go rummaging around for the hammer, when all at once out flies the boss screaming, 'She's getting up!' and hightails it across the fields. Anyway, I held onto that hammer—it made me feel better—and went inside. I don't mind telling you, my hair practically stood up on end. It's a good thing I had that hammer in my hand. But what do you have on Saturday?"

"Mixed grill with pommes frites and Linzer torte. But what about . . ."

"But what about the soup, Eman? What kind of soup do you have?"

"Tripe, tripe soup. Now tell me, what happened next?"

"So I go in, and there's Franta leaning over the bed and pushing down the corpse's knees, and she seems to be trying to get up."

"And what did you do?"

"I screamed. And Franta turned around, jumped up, pushed me out of the doorway, and disappeared. But I held onto that hammer; it made me feel better."

"You took it like a man."

"That's what everybody said. Say, what do they give the people with Sunday shifts?"

"When? What? Oh, Sunday. Schnitzel à la parisienne. But tell me . . ."

"And the soup?"

"Beef noodle with hunks of meat floating around in it. Go on and eat now, or your soup'll get cold."

"Let's see now . . . noodle soup. I like noodle soup. With hunks of meat floating in it?"

"Big hunks of meat."

"You're not trying to pull my leg now, are you?"

"Of course not. Big hunks of meat."

"Well then, I believe you. So anyway, I went up to the bed and looked that corpse right in the face. You know, she looked like a cradle, her legs tucked under her and all. That's the kind of thing that happens to you when you're old and forgotten and you die alone in cold weather. You roll up into a little ball, and what can you do when there's no one to straighten you out again? If I die in the cold, there'll be no one to straighten me out either. I'm all alone myself."

"But what about your children? Didn't you say you had seven children?"

"Oh, that's true enough. But not one of them keeps in touch."

"You know what? I'll ask my mother to have a look in on you now and then."

"Eman, it's been real good of you to come sit here with me and talk about all that food. Life has taught me things you can't find in books, and I know your kind. You can be a real pest when you want to be. But at least you have a little feeling for people. . . . So your mother's going to look in on me from time to time, eh?"

"I'll ask her to. You can be sure of that. Good night now."

"Good night," she mumbled, "good night," and slowly sipped her soup.

THE DEATH OF MR. BALTISBERGER

Nearly the whole morning and then again after lunch they had lain under the car on some old sacks fixing the rear springs.

"I wonder how that spring got busted?" asked Father, annoyed.

"How? It all happened that night on our way home," said Uncle Pepin, who was holding the light. "'Uncle Pepin,' Slávek says to me, 'we've all got to die sometime. Here's the wheel. You take over.' So I did, even though I'm over seventy and can't see any too good. And you know what? We didn't even go off the road more than two or three times."

"Well, you won't catch me loaning you the car any more. Just look at it! How many of you were there?"

"Not all that many. Only six. But the worst part was the bottom falling out. We had to put the bottom on the roof, on top of the bed."

"What bed?"

"The bed we were moving for the butcher. The butcher was inside the car, though."

"Oh no," Father wailed. "I was wondering where those scratches on the roof came from. No, sir, you won't catch me lending you my car any more." And he took the wrench and gave the car such a whack that a mess of dried mud flew in his eyes. But that was just before the Grand Prix, so they changed the broken spring in a hurry and wired a folding garden chair to where the back seat used to be. Because a long

157

time ago, five years back, Father had started to spruce up the old Škoda 430. He had torn out the upholstery, then the seats, and stored them away in the shed, and for five years he and Mother had dreamed of how someday they'd wash and clean it all up, invest a few hundred in the body, and make the old jalopy respectable again.

Whenever we went anywhere, people would say, "Say, she's looking a bit under the weather, your highboy there. You sure you didn't hide her in the Elbe during the war?" And Father would get annoyed because he really had hidden her in the Elbe. Another question people were always asking is, "How come everybody in the car looks like they're sitting in a bathtub?" The answer was that there were no seats and the passengers sat on margarine crates. But this was all just temporary, because all that Father saw was his perpetual vision: a beautiful, well-appointed Škoda 430.

So for the Grand Prix of Czechoslovakia they put two upholstered armchairs in the front and wired a folding chair from the garden in the back. Mother fried up a stack of schnitzel and filled an old vinegar bottle with bitters, and shortly after midnight they set off for Brno and the motorcycle races.

After they'd finished the schnitzel in the beautiful countryside, Father fell asleep, and Mother and Uncle Pepin stretched out at the edge of the woods, next to the Farina curves, to follow the races—with time out for an occasional swig from the vinegar bottle. The 150 category was in its last lap with Franta Bartoš—calm, collected, and hunched down low over the handlebars of his OHC—far out in front. As he thundered around the track, 250,000 spectators would rise in waves and cheer, and he could see it all—all those hands and scarves and handkerchiefs, all that glory. He wasn't scared, not Franta

Bartoš; he was never afraid of anything, except maybe of a sparkplug conking out on him, or a burned-out piston. Now he was rounding the last of the Farina curves. He never even let up on the gas. All he did was hunch forward a bit lower and move right along.

Uncle Pepin, who could not see very well, kept up a steady stream of banter. "Last year I went to see what shape the archbishop's old residence was in. The orchard was empty, nothing but leaves and an old woman sitting there crunching away on the apples. If the late Archbishop Kohn had caught her, the old hag would have gotten a few well-placed kicks for putting down her broom. He was a nervous one all right, especially when he was young and the forester took a shot at him for playing around with his wife. Finally the archbishop moved to the Tyrol with his cook to be nearer to God."

In the meanwhile Mother had struck up a conversation with a man in a wheel chair whose family had wheeled him up there on Saturday night because the track closed before midnight.

Uncle Pepin walked over to the wheel chair and said, "I had a view very much like this one, one night I was out walking with a clever little looker. Heda was her name. And this Heda said to me, she said, 'Will you walk me to the cemetery?' And so I did. I was the handsomest fellow far and wide. I felt just like an artist. It was so exciting with her all dressed in white like a queen saying, 'Isn't it all just too romantic?' Well, I led her across some bumpy old paths and up a little hill. The same kind of terrain they have here. A lot like Dolnja Tuzla in Bosnia and Herzegovina, too. Anyway, Heda sat down on a rock and said, 'What have you been doing with yourself? You're never around any more.' And I told her my heart was aching so she'd think I was the type who writes poetry. Anyway, she put her parasol down on the rock and lay down on her back and looked up at the sky, and my spine started tingling. And then she said, 'You know, my mother likes you a lot. Why don't you come and have dinner with us?' But I didn't say anything, because her brother had syphilis. So then she said to me, 'I can't seem to catch my breath! Oh, how I wish I were dead and buried!' And I agreed with her and consoled her with the thought that poets say the most beautiful thing in the world is a dead beauty."

But the man in the wheel chair was looking deep into Mother's eyes and seemed upset. "It's a crying shame Mandolini cut up his face during warm-ups! He would have shown that Bartoš a thing or two!"

"Come on!" said Mother, unwilling to give in. "The way Bartoš is driving today, he would have beaten your Mandolini hands down!"

"How can you say that! How can you sit there and say that!" cried the man in the wheel chair.

"It's the truth. That's how." She took another swig from the vinegar bottle.

"We'll see," said the cripple, wiggling in his chair. "The 350s will show you. Wait till you see how Mr. Baltisberger leaves them all behind. Štastný included!"

"Is Baltisberger a German?" asked Uncle Pepin.

"That's right," said the man quietly, smoothing out the blanket he was sitting on.

"Then he's bound to win, because the Germans are a pack of bastards. One day Dr. Karafiát, the leader of our Sokol gymnastics group, a freethinker—he wore a pince-nez—and an elegant bachelor like yours truly, took us through a German village on our way home from practice. And as we were walking along I asked him why he had never gotten married. You know what he said? 'A real man is an ornament of nature. That makes him refined. And who can be refined with a woman parading around the room waving his chamber pot!' So there we were, walking through that German village singing patriotic Czech songs, never suspecting that our dear neighbors were waiting in ambush around the bend. Just as we started 'The Lion's Height, the Eagle's Flight,' out those sons of bitches flew. They pulled Dr. Karafiát off his horse and clubbed us black and blue. The doctor's eye swelled up something awful. His nose was broken too. I used to go to him for my eyes."

"Baltisberger's got a big heart," interrupted the cripple, and banged his cane on the blanket.

"Which means that Štastný doesn't?" said Mother, raising her eyes.

"Who said he doesn't? But it's like he's going so fast out of spite. It scares the hell out of me."

"How right you are," nodded Uncle Pepin. "Spite's a bad thing, a very bad thing. Take Ferdinand, the one who was going to be emperor; now he was full of spite too. A big son of a bitch too, with a butt like the broad side of a barn. Why, he would have needed a throne like Maria Theresa's, a throne as big as a well. Whenever he found women gathering firewood on the estate at Konopiště, he'd set fire to it right on their backs. And once he knocked the gardener's head against the wall just because he found a cracked flowerpot in the green-house."

"There, you see?" said the cripple to Mother. "And are the Bavarians ever going to knock your Štastný for a loop in the 500 category! Klinger and Peter Knees, both of them. Yesterday morning at warm-ups I saw Štastný take such a spill on a 500 that I thought he was done for. He must have been doing a good eighty-five. But you've got to hand it to him; that Štastný sure knows how to go down with his machine. I can't deny that. And let me tell you: going down with your cycle is an art. Of course, he's had his share of bad luck. And besides, he's never found a machine to suit him yet. One that can keep pace with his spite. Normally it's the machine that wears out the rider, but with Mr. Štastný it's the other way around. And what guts. No one has more guts than Šťastný. Nobody, I swear."

"Just like the villagers from the next town, they had guts too," put in Uncle Pepin. "When they got called up to fight in the war, they beat the hell out of every last German, including the burgomeister. They herded them all into the brewery and rammed a knife in the burgomeister's neck for good measure."

"Glad to hear it," said the cripple. "After all, who is in a better position than me to know what makes a heart big? I rode a Harley with one leg. But when I lost the other one . . ." He spoke bitterly, lifting both hands and letting them drop back onto the wheel chair's black armrests.

"I'm sorry," whispered Mother.

"Forget it. But let me tell you something funny. One day I had my brother in the sidecar. My left leg was gone by that time, and I had an iron leg instead. As we were riding along the sidecar tore loose, and because I was leaning my iron leg up against the pin that held the sidecar onto the motorcycle, both the leg and my lederhosen came off with the sidecar. My brother slid into the ditch at the side of the road, and I took an easy spill. But my leg took a flying leap and landed in the road, right in front of two women on their way home from market. One of them fainted dead away as soon as she set eyes on it. But since I wasn't hurt at all, I hopped out onto the road for my other leg. And just as I bent down for it, the braver of the two women bit the dust. Things weren't so bad with one leg, but now? All I am is a crabby old man."

He looked off into the distance and pulled himself up so unnaturally straight in his wheel chair that Uncle Pepin took to comforting him. "Jesus Christ and our own home-grown Havlíček were in the same boat. Neither of them ever cracked a smile either, and they were both as handsome as they come. If you've got a mission in this world, you can't fool around.

Havlíček's brain was as sharp as a diamond. Why, even the professors had to hand it to him. . . ."

"That's all well and good," replied the man in the wheel chair, "but just keep in mind that the Grand Prix isn't what it used to be. Two years ago when that Australian Campbell won, they had a party for the participants, and I wheeled over there too, and when they asked for questions, I had them translate mine for him: 'What's it like to race with George Geoffrey Duke, Mr. Campbell?' I asked him. And the Australian said that Duke was the best racer of all time and that his, Campbell's, greatest achievement was to finish half a lap behind him. And all the fans started clapping and yelling, 'Hurray for Duke!' "

"It's people like that make the world go round! Take my friend Římský," said Uncle Pepin, all excited. "Nobody dared look in his direction, let alone try to talk to him. Once we were having a beer, fifty people in the place, and someone started pushing me around. Well, my friend Římský smashed the table to smithereens, tore down the lights, and in no time flat the whole place was a shambles. By the time it was over four policemen had died in the hospital, the rest jumped out the window, and while Římský was kicking away at their spiked helmets, he kicked the wooden leg off of one of the waitresses who had gotten mixed up in it. He didn't stop thrashing until they called the fire brigade and hosed him straight in the eyes. But in jail he revived: he sawed through his chains—and those chains were strong enough for an ox—broke down the doorframe, and gave the guards a beating with the beams."

"Yes, that kind of people are still around!" cried the cripple who had ridden a Harley when only one of his legs was left. "Just imagine what it would be like if our Grand Prix was declared part of the world championship. Wouldn't that be something! Ubbiali on an Augusta in Brno! Bill Lomas on a Guzzi!

And all the others—John Surtees and Armstrong and maybe even George Geoffrey Duke himself—here in Brno! What a race that would make!"

"Just like when Archbishop Kohn came to visit," said Uncle Pepin. "He was a Wallachian of Jewish descent, with hair like flax, a golden pince-nez, and a ring on his finger worth several million. He smelled of royal musk, like a barmaid, and the aroma followed him around like smoke follows a locomotive." He stopped to take a breath, and went on. "Anyway, when he came to visit, all the old women wanted to kiss his hands. But the deacons kept shoving them away; they didn't want his sleeves to get slobbered over. Of course, the notary's daughters from the castle kissed the hands of the archbishop himself. Archbishop Stojan, on the other hand, yes, there was a goodhearted soul. A beggar could be dead drunk and he'd still get a gold coin. Now Archbishop Bauer—he was an ugly one. Nothing but warts and blue blood. Very unpleasant for confirmations. But then again, his face frightened so many people during extreme unction, a couple of them got scared right out of it and got better. And Archbishop Perčan, he was always helping people. He once took my mother's hand and said to her, 'May the good Lord bless you and keep you, and I hope you don't get trampled to death on your way out.' And along with his blessing he gave her a gold coin, because he loved his women, the mainstay of the Church. He also loved to give sermons on why a Christian shouldn't have the smell of liquor on his breath when he goes to church. Of course, nearly all these archbishops were champs when it came to food. That Prečan polished off a whole basket of squabs in one sitting, and Bauer, he downed half a keg of beer and had a whole suckling pig for lunch."

While Uncle Pepin was talking, the 350 race had begun, and just as he finished, František Šťastný thundered around the bend, out in the lead on his Jawa OHC.

"Is that Štastný, the one with the red bandana?" asked Mother.

"That's him, all right," answered the cripple when the first group and their earsplitting machines had disappeared into the woods.

Mother put her arms around one of the birch trees and leaned as far forward as she could so as to catch them coming into the curve. Her heart beat fast as the red bandana streaked by.

"Look how he holds himself!" she said.

"Oh, he knows how to hold himself, all right," said the cripple. "It doesn't surprise me in the least that during the first few heats at Zandvoort those Dutchmen couldn't figure out whether it was a madman or what it was they had on the track. But when they realized that Štastný knew what he was up to and had class to boot, they went wild over him. All the same, though, I'll take Baltisberger any day."

"Take him or leave him; it's who wins that counts," said Uncle Pepin. "We once had a race too—with the fire engines. The mill was on fire, and our horses went so wild we had to pull the fire engines to the fire ourselves. There we were, sweating like mules. I stood at the edge of the pond with the suction pump waiting for the commander to blow his trumpet the way it says in the rule book. But instead of a trumpet he blew a tin can, so the firemen gave me a shove, and I forgot to let go of the pump and went flying into the water, and the firemen had to fish me out with poles because I didn't know how to swim. I joined the fire brigade because a pretty girl once told me I'd look good with an ax and ladder. Then we had to fish the pump out with our hooks, and by that time half the mill had burned down. We finally got the pump to work and were just about to start pumping when I got tangled up in one of the hooks, because I was groggy from falling into the water, and the pump handle hit me on the head so hard I passed out.

So then they had to take time out to bring me around, and they lost so much time that the fire brigade from the other town got their water going first. And even after the mill had burned to the ground I got a bawling out from the commander for lousing our side up."

Just then there was an announcement from the loudspeaker in the branches that Baltisberger was having exhaust trouble and that Hinton was trailing Štastný by a full minute. Štastný kept up the pace as if they were both still on his neck. He gave her everything he had on the straightaway and hit the curves at 120 mph. Then he would hold back ever so slightly, and as soon as he was out of the last curves, zoom, he'd step on it so hard that the spectators didn't have time to clap or cheer. All they could do was tremble. Štastný was running so wild he seemed either out of his mind or hell bent on vengeance.

"I certainly hope his sparkplugs hold out," said Mother, letting out her breath and taking another swig from the bottle of bitters.

"Baltisberger was a little too sure of himself. I could tell from the way he took that first lap. He looked too proud," replied the cripple.

"That's the way it always is," said Uncle Pepin. "I had a religion teacher, a giant, six five, six six, and he once asked us to define the Holy Trinity. And one kid answered, 'Holy Trinity is the little sister of Holy Mary.' Well, the priest picked him up like a rabbit, shook him back and forth a few times, gave him a few punches in the nose, and then banged his head against the blackboard, because in those days we followed the teachings of that noble Czech John Amos Comenius, who said a pupil must never be proud and the rod must never be spared."

"He's a good two minutes ahead by now," said Mother, corking up the bottle.

Štastný was heading into the curves with even more accuracy

and daring than before. He wasn't riding for the crowd any more; he was riding for himself. He almost seemed to be riding for the pleasure of doing something the way it ideally ought to be done and for the joy of whistling along on the border line between life and death. Fate was with him. He could feel it in his every move. The spectators began to perk up too when they saw how confident he looked. In the last lap he rode through sort of a tunnel, a valley of shouts, hands, handkerchiefs, and everything else that you can use to express enthusiasm. As soon as he rounded the bend, seats turned into standing room.

During the intermission before the 250 race, Mother woke up Father, who had slept through everything up to that point.

"Get up and come have a look. It's fun."

Father took a drink of the bitters and said, "Fun? Motorcycles? Now if it was *car* racing: Hermann Lang, Rudolf Caracciola, Tazio Nuvolari, five-liter displacement, three superchargers! Now that was something to look at. It didn't surprise me a bit to hear Rudolf Caracciola say that his life begins when he hears the roar of the engines."

The man in the wheel chair asked almost humbly, "You mean you know Caracciola?"

"I do," said Father. "I stood beside him at his wife's funeral. She was buried alive by an avalanche in the Alps. You should have seen him in training. One tiny glass of champagne, and only after he won a race."

"Have you ever seen one of the big races?"

"I have," said Father. "And let me tell you, I don't even like to think about it! It was the Grand Prix of Tripoli. A dog ran out onto the track in front of Varzi and that was that. Achilles Varzi died in the crash." He told it exactly the way he had read it in the books Caracciola and Hans von Stuck had written about it. "And then I saw the tragic Monza Grand Prix warmup session where Borzacchini and Campari were killed when they skidded on some oil lost by a single seater. An hour later Czajkowski went under on the same spot. They all flew off the cliff into the sea, each one of them. I was in the cigar store just beneath the rock where they laid out the corpses. The owner of the shop told me that several of the crowned heads of Europe had lain up there on that rock."

"You mean you knew Borzacchini?"

"No, but in the hotel I once saw him turn on the fan, toss up all the money he had won, and dance his way through the fluttering bank notes."

"That's just the kind of thing Baron Königsvater's son would do!" cried Uncle Pepin. "Old Königsvater was made a baron by the Emperor even though his grandfather used to peddle shoelaces from village to village. He lived in a castle and raised horses, and he had mirrors in his stables so the horses could look at themselves while they ate and get more enjoyment out of their meals. His son married a starving actress though, and did they have one hell of a good time together, until one day the family fortune gave out. And when the old baron heard about it he had a heart attack and died."

"That makes a fine story, but tell me: what do you think is the best car on the market: Mercedes, Maserati, or Alfa Romeo?"

"As far as I'm concerned, it's the good old Czech Škoda 430," replied Father without a moment's hesitation. "It's dependable, it's nice and warm inside, and it's easy to drive. What's more, you can load five hundred pounds of potatoes in it without any trouble. Last week we had six people on the inside and a large cabinet on top." He looked over in the direction where he thought the car was parked.

"Attention!" announced the loudspeaker in the trees. "The 250 race is assembling at the starting line. Before we begin, please note the following changes in your programs. For Autengruber, Austria, substitute Andersson, Sweden—both on Nortons. For . . . Attention! Twenty seconds, fifteen, ten seconds, five . . . the 250 race is on!"

The roaring motors gradually grew in intensity.

"Baltisberger is out in front. He is traveling at an incredible speed. Hot on his tail, also on an NSU Sport-Max, we have Kassner, and behind Baltisberger and Kassner, that good-natured Australian, Brown, with the kangaroo on his helmet. On level ground they are approaching speeds of 125 mph."

Hans Baltisberger was the first to shoot up to the Farina curves. He was going so fast that Mother saw nothing but a silver streak. Then Brown, and an instant later Kassner. All they left behind was the aroma of burned gas.

"Hans may be ahead, but there's something wrong, something wrong. It's a spiteful ride, all or nothing," said the cripple, tapping his cane against his false leg.

"Something can always go wrong," said Uncle Pepin. "Once we were on maneuvers and the late Emperor Franz Josef and his uncle Albrecht, the one with the buck teeth, came to see us. After maneuvers there was a mass in church, and I didn't go, because I was up to my ears in freethinking at the time. But all of a sudden a thunderstorm came up and a flash of lightning hit the lightning rod, slid down into the choir loft, and knocked the organist unconscious. Well, the women got all hysterical and made for the sacristy, but the priest kicked them all out and gave it to the sacristan for letting the women in when he, God's proxy on earth, was in his underwear. So then they headed for the altar, and there the panic really got out of hand. You see, the women thought the ceiling was falling, but all that was actually happening was that the sacristan, who had been ringing the storm bell, had given the rope too hard a yank, and down it came, whistling and lashing out at the women's heads and even laying a few of them low."

"Hans Baltisberger is still in the lead, with Kassner at his heels," announced the loudspeaker system. "Bartoš has developed engine trouble and is out of the race. Attention, all officials! The stretch leading up to the Farina curves has reported strong side winds and moderate shower activity."

"That's all we needed," sighed the man in the wheel chair. As the main group drew near, he was afraid to look, but then he couldn't resist staring, and when they had shot by, he had the feeling he would never see them again. "This is no race; it's a torture chamber."

"Oh, but that's life," said Uncle Pepin, trying to console him. "Two girls from a bar tried to poison themselves on account of me. The first one's name was Vlasta, and Vlasta said to me, 'Do it with me for love.' But I told her I had pains in my chest. So she got angry and said, 'Come on, you crumb, or do I have to hit you over the head with a bottle?' But that was a good sign, because that Vlasta could really make men go for her. Then along came a group of butchers, and I did some of my acrobatic stunts for them, and we all had such a good time that the doctor had to come and have a look at Vlasta and the police had to take me home in a cart like a roll of linoleum."

"What about the other one?"

"Well, she tried to poison herself with slivovitz. She was always laughing, and her name was Zdenka. Once she started kissing me right in the bar, and the dragoon lieutenants almost went crazy. Then she took me to her room, and I told her about how Mozart is supernatural. But she comforted me with 'Cut the crap. The only way you'll get anywhere with me is if you're a man.' So we lay down on the bed, and I thought of jumping out the window, but her room was on the second floor. Anyway, Zdenka snuggled up to me and said I was free to do with her as I pleased. So I told her about how when Strauss first saw the score for Mozart's *Jupiter* he said, 'I feel sick.' And Zdenka answered, 'Well, so do I! What about my body?' I thought of making a break for it out the door, but there was a St.

Bernard growling in the hallway. So I sang a few lines from 'Hear My Song, Violette,' and gave in."

At that moment the motorcycles were rounding the bend again, and again Hans Baltisberger, No. 3, was out in front. Mother saw him look around to see how far back the others were, and just then he skidded. His front wheel flew up in the air, the silver NSU Sport-Max rammed into a telephone pole, and the whole thing disappeared in the ditch by the side of the road. Then Kassner thundered by, taking the curves every bit as fast as he had the lap before.

"All you young sports fans!" croaked the loudspeaker. "Try your skill, try your luck at your local tracks. One moment, please. We have a report here that Kassner has taken over the lead. Whatever could have happened to Baltisberger, No. 3?"

"I knew it. I just felt it was going to happen," said the man in the wheel chair, trying to raise himself up on his hands. "I've always got to be there when something like this happens. Farina hit the dust right here before my very eyes. Prinz Biro sailed into the stands right next to where I was sitting. I'm just always on the spot when something like this happens."

Father got up.

"Don't go," said Mother. But Father ran through the trees to the underpass and across to the other side of the road, where he saw them turning Mr. Baltisberger over on his back.

Pointing to the stump of a tree, a young man said, "That's where he hit his head."

Father was calm. He kneeled down next to Mr. Baltisberger and helped the nurse pull off his helmet. They had a hard time; shattered as he was, the racer kept trying to stand up and somehow slip out of his body. His efforts were in vain, though, for suddenly he collapsed and began spitting blood.

"*Ich bitte . . . Ich grüsse . . .*" he whispered.

Then his head fell to one side and a quiver went through his exposed nerves. When the sun came out, his blood sparkled like rippling rubies.

"Horst Kassner is still out in front," came the voice of the loudspeaker through the wet leaves, "followed by Heck, both on NSU's. Kvěch and Koštýř, on CZ's, are working their way up. Ladies and gentlemen, what a beautiful sight! A helicopter, light and elegant as a dragonfly, has just taken off. What a shame the aerial view isn't being carried on television! Will all spectators kindly keep their distance. Before the helicopter lands, it will drop several hundred fliers to remind you that next Sunday is Air Day."

Father looked at his watch.

It said one forty-eight.

Then the doctor came. He first held Mr. Baltisberger's wrist and then bent over his chest. By the time he stood up again his face wore an on-the-job expression. Father realized that Mr. Baltisberger was dead.

"He's somebody's son," he said to himself, picking up the helmet and placing it on the wreck of the machine.

Horst Kassner shot by. He must have figured out what had happened, that Baltisberger was dead, but far from letting up, he seemed to want to pay homage to his friend by lighting into those curves the way the dead man used to: with daring, accuracy, and the very highest speed the machine, his heart, and his cool brain would allow.

The nurse began winding a bandage around Baltisberger's head, but the more she wound, the more red seeped through.

"Any moment now we'll have our winner. Will it be Kassner or Heck? Our helicopter is rising higher and higher. At a hundred and fifty feet, at three hundred feet, it's still dropping those fliers. And now . . . here they come: it's Kassner first. Then . . . yes, Heck! Both on elegant machines that look for all the world like silver swans."

When Mother told Uncle Pepin that Mr. Baltisberger had

been killed, his reaction was: "A pity I'm not any younger. I'd climb on one of those noisemakers and show them a thing or two. I served with the most beautiful army in the world, you know. In those days, soldiers wore laced corsets the way the ladies used to. Once I borrowed a uniform from a cadet. Oh, that patent leather belt! I had my hair curled with a curling iron, and the local photographer took my picture. I had a beautiful complexion, just like my cousin, who was in the Emperor's Guard. He was a big hulk of a guy, but later he took to drink. Still, when he was young, he had the most beautiful body in the district. He weighed way over two hundred pounds, and when he took off his clothes his body was as white as the fallen snow, and they called him Pretty František. My picture hung in the main square, and once, when there was a crowd of girls in front of the photographer's window, I heard one of them ask, 'Who do you like the best?' And the girl she asked pointed to me. Well, I was standing behind her and I don't mind telling you I went home on cloud nine."

While Uncle Pepin was talking, the man in the wheel chair sat with his head down, the tears dropping down on his blanket. . . .

On the other side of the trees, three or four hundred yards beyond the Farina curves, two young apprentices had just woken up. Like tens of thousands of other fans, they had driven all night to come to the races, and like tens of thousands of other fans, they had walked around Brno in the early morning hours and returned to the track shortly after seven to yell and scream over Bartoš's victory and marvel at Štastný's daring. But by that time they were so tired that during the intermission they had stretched out, spread their coats over themselves, and fallen asleep.

"It's your fault! It was all your idea."

"Me? You were the one that said just for a while."

"Maybe I did, but why did you have to take me up on it?"

"You're the sleepyhead."

"You're the one who can never get up in the morning. I'll kill myself if we slept through Baltisberger."

They stopped arguing long enough to run up to the track.

"Is the 250 race over?" they asked the first passer-by.

"Yes, it is."

"Who came in first?"

"Kassner."

"And second?"

"Heck."

"Third?"

"Koštýř."

"But what about Baltisberger?"

"He made the last turn of his life up there by the Farina curves. I can't say I recommend the sight, boys."

But since they had come all this way to get a look at him, they set off right away through the underpass. Then they saw it: a body under a tarpaulin and—a few steps away, also sticking out from under a tarpaulin—an NSU Sport-Max. At that point a beige Mercedes pulled up quietly. It was the same one they had admired in front of the Hotel Morava that morning. Out jumped a mechanic. He ran down into the ditch and with two fingers touched the tarpaulin at the spot he thought the head should be. Then he took off the helmet and hit it against the stump of a tree to knock the dried blood out.

"Horst Kassner has mounted the victors' podium, with Heck to his right, Koštýř to his left," came the announcement through the loudspeaker. "Three little Pioneer girls are tying their red kerchiefs around the winners' necks. The helicopter has climbed so high it is lost in the sun. And now please note the following change in your programs: for No. 8, Bill Hall, Great Britain, substitute Czekurti, Hungary, on a Giller. Before the 500 race begins, substitute . . ."

"Is Mr. Baltisberger really dead?" asked one of the apprentices sadly.

THE WORLD CAFETERIA

The silver streams of an evening shower streamed down the cafeteria's plate-glass front. A few people made their way across the tiny square, leaning into the rain and clutching their hats or umbrellas.

Boisterous music and conversations, occasionally breaking into wild laughter, filtered down from the mezzanine lounge. The woman at the tap drew a last stein and went to the ladies' room.

Opening the door, she saw a pair of perforated shoes hanging three or four feet off the ground, then a pair of legs sticking out of a yellow and red plaid skirt, and finally a jacket with a pair of limp arms in the sleeves and a girl's head drooping over the lapel.

The girl was hanging by the belt of her trench coat from the latch of the ventilator window.

"Well, well," said the tap woman, and went for a ladder. A waitress held the body steady while the tap woman cut it down with a long salami knife. Then she heaved it over her shoulder, carried it around to an alcove in back of the counter, laid it out on the dirty-dish table, and loosened the belt.

When she looked up, there was a man standing out in the rain on the other side of the cafeteria's plate-glass front, staring in at the table. The tap woman drew the chintz curtains.

Then the ambulance came. A young doctor ran into the cafeteria, while two orderlies pulled a stretcher out of the back of the vehicle. The doctor put his ear up to the girl's chest, felt her pulse, pulled open the curtain, and made a sign to the orderlies to stop.

"There's nothing we can do," he said.

"But what about us? What do we do with her?" asked the waitress.

"That's for pathology to decide."

"Well, I hope your pathology gets here soon. We sell food and drinks in this place."

"Then you'd better close up for a while," said the doctor, running out into the rain. The ambulance lurched forward with a wail. Boisterous music and conversations, occasionally breaking into wild laughter, filtered down from the mezzanine lounge. By now a group of curious onlookers had gathered in front of the window. They were leaning their hands up against the glass, and their palms looked white and unnaturally large. Just above the hands shone a row of inquisitive eyes.

A tall young man came up to the door. He was soaking wet, and his sleeves were white from bumping against the plaster-covered walls. He tried the door and was about to go away, when the tap woman went over and unlocked it for him.

"Come on in. Come on in and cheer me up," she said. But when he was safely in she threw up her hands in dismay. "What's happened to you? Did you get run over by a train? Or fall off a cliff?"

"Worse," he said. "It's my fiancée: she ran out on me two days ago."

"You mean you're engaged? Why, I've never even seen you with a girl." As she talked, she swished empty glasses around in the sink, filled them with beer, loaded them into the dumb-waiter behind her, pulled down the cover, and pushed the button. Then she picked up one of the steins and sent it sailing down the wet tin surface of the counter. It stopped right under the young man's hand.

He took a drink, scraped his foot on the brass footrail, and watched the water trickle off his shoe.

"Ran away," he said. "We were having some stale crusts for dinner, when she suddenly remembered the barons in her background. 'Karlík,' she screamed at me, 'Karlík, I'd like to stick a hand grenade in your mother's kisser.' But instead she took a knife, one of those fancy pocket-knife jobs, and rammed it into the door. Well, the knife snapped shut and she cut herself, and I ran to close the window so she wouldn't throw herself out. That girl has suicide on the brain."

"Stale crusts for dinner?" asked the waitress in surprise.

"That's right. And you know, she wanted us to make it a double suicide. 'Look, Karlík,' she said to me, 'let's open the window, hold hands, and jump.' So we each took a bath and put on our Sunday best, and I looked down into our chasm of a courtyard to make sure we wouldn't land on some little kid, and what did I see but a stupid antenna sticking out of a second-floor window, so if we jumped from the fourth floor where we live, we would certainly have cut off an ear or a nose on the wire, and then think what we'd have looked like." The beer dribbled along his mouth like a wispy mustache.

"But how can anybody possibly care what they're going to look like afterward?" asked the tap woman, folding her arms, looking as beautiful as the statue on the Ministry of Agriculture building.

Boisterous music and conversations, occasionally breaking into wild laughter, filtered down from the mezzanine lounge.

"I am an aesthete. Need I say more? Of course my girl, she couldn't have cared less. Once she tried to strangle herself with the belt of a trenchcoat, and I only just got her down in time. 'You moron,' she yelled. 'What did you bring me back for? I was already in limbo!' Well, the neighbors began banging on the walls and yelling, 'What's going on in there? Don't forget there are children present.' And my fiancée yelled back, 'You know what I'd like to do to your children? I'd like to slit their throats and then set fire to this dump!' So, to calm her down, I grabbed one arm and one leg and was all set to spin her around, but I miscalculated and sent her flying headfirst through the door and out into the hall, where she knocked over the neighbor who had been kneeling down by the keyhole. And you know what she said to that woman?" he asked with a smile. "She said, 'Lady, Karlík and I can do whatever we please in the confines of our own home, can't we, Karlík?'" His eyes were rimmed with red, like a telegram form.

"Why, that's awful," said the tap woman. "Just look at them. Why, that bunch of no-goods has even brought along their own stools." She drew herself a small beer and walked over to the large plate-glass window. Dozens of onlookers—some replete with stools—had gathered out front in the pouring rain. They were whispering to one another and pressing their hands up against the glass as if it could keep them warm. They looked like monsters.

The tap woman took a gulp of the beer, bent forward until she was almost wearing the window like a pair of glasses, then leaned back again, and pitched the rest of the beer against the transparent wall. The foam trickled down the glass-covered portraits.

"That's Prague for you," she said with a shrug of the shoulders.

Back at the tap, she drew a couple of steins and sent one more sailing down the wet tin surface of the counter. Again it stopped right under the young man's hand.

"Why do I always have to be around when something goes wrong?" she said. "Last year I was out for a little walk along the tracks, when I see this girl walking toward me. Along comes the train, and the girl jumps right under the locomotive. Then her head rolls down the embankment, lands at my feet—and winks at me!"

But the young man was as deeply immersed in himself as a collapsible sewing machine. "I'll never let her go," he said. "If nothing else, she's done a great service for Czech graphic art by being frigid. What if I'd had a normal woman? Sure we'd have made love, but that would have been the end of absolute graphics."

He raised his glass; the beer ran down his shirt.

Boisterous music and conversations, occasionally breaking into wild laughter, filtered down from the mezzanine lounge. Trayloads of empty glasses coated with dried foam rode down from the restaurant in the dumbwaiter.

"You know, my girl always used to tell me I was out of my mind, but how could I be crazy and still go to work and have hands that can draw bodies and brakes for jet planes with an accuracy of plus or minus a hundredth of a millimeter?"

"That beats everything!" shouted the waitress in a rage.

A group of onlookers was now perched on the slippery, resilient boughs of a linden tree, hanging onto the branches above like passengers on a tram. They had a bird's-eye view of the entire cafeteria, including the chintz curtain, now slightly open, behind which the corpse lay on the dirty-dish table.

"Why do I always have to be around when there's trouble?" complained the waitress. "One dark night I stopped on my way home for a call of nature, and as I'm feeling my way out of the bushes I grab hold of this cold hand. I light a match and hold it up, and there's this guy hanging there, sticking his tongue out at me. Say, it's really pouring out." She looked up over the heads of onlookers to the street lamps. The wind had opened up the locust branches, and an illuminated clock-face on the building across the square peeked through.

Boisterous music and conversations, occasionally breaking into wild laughter, filtered down from the mezzanine lounge.

A young man in shabby-looking work clothes appeared at the door and held up a crate of empty beer steins. The waitress unlocked the door and began filling them.

"What's a handsome guy like you go around dressed like that for?"

"That's the way we dress at the factory. It's our style," said the mechanic. "On our way to work we look like anybody else, but you ought to see us on the job. There was a time when patched coveralls were the rage. Our guys managed to come up with more patches than a hobo masquerade. Another time, the thing to do was to wear your coveralls tied together with wire, and the whole plant tinkled like a puppet show. The latest fad is beat-up shoes." And he showed her a work shoe with bronze wire shoelace and no sole at all. "And one of the pants legs has to be either run over or mangled by a gear wheel." He stepped back to model.

"Very fancy," said the waitress admiringly as she put the filled steins back into the crate.

"The girls who come to work looking like movie stars wear rubber boots with flapping soles," said the young man, his wet, wavy carrot top gleaming like copper buckles. "Say, what are those people waiting for out there in the rain?"

"There's a big wedding going on upstairs," she said, looking up to the ceiling. Then, with the eye of a true connoisseur, she watched the handsome mechanic stretch out his one suspender with his thumb.

When he had gone, she turned and asked the young man, "How about you? Still like your work at the factory?"

"You bet," said the young man. "I can't live without my work—just like I can't live without my girl. Do you know that the plant where I work sponsored my first exhibition?" he said proudly. "My own factory! First I had to argue it out with the guy in charge of cultural activities, but finally he told me to set it up at night. So late one night I broke in and tacked up the whole thing: Tactile Experiences on the Job. When that cultural guy saw them the next morning, he practically had a breakdown. Then there was a little bit of an argument and I tore one of his sleeves off, but the exhibition went on all the same. The guys at the plant really liked it. For the opening we invited a chorus of blind children. They stood facing a sign that stretched from one end of the balcony to the other. WE MUST DEFEND OUR UNITY LIKE THE APPLE OF OUR EYE. And now the plant is always boasting of how I had my first exhibit right there at the plant."

And boisterous music and conversations, occasionally breaking into wild laughter, filtered down from the mezzanine lounge.

The bride, wearing a white veil, was the first to come downstairs. She was young, and her eyes shone from the alcohol as she turned and led the bridegroom down the steps. The ushers and bridesmaids all held firmly onto the banister, trying not to trip on her train. The bride was singing and beating time with her bouquet, and having finally reached the bottom of the stairs, she burst into the glass corridor, shouted something at the onlookers, and then ran out into the silver wickerwork of the rain. Once outside, she spread her arms wide, tipped back her head, and let her hair and bridal wreath go limp in the downpour. The water made her clothes cling to the lines of her lovely body. The bridegroom and the rest of the bridal party soon joined her with whoops of joy. They crossed single file to the other side of the street. The bride led the procession, twirling the stem of her bouquet and beating time for the songs and marching. "A happy wedding. The way they ought to be," said the tap woman, sliding down off a beer bottle crate. "But tell me, was it yesterday you said your fiancée ran out on you?"

"No, the day before yesterday," he said, rubbing a red eye, "and you know, it doesn't surprise me in the least. All that girl reads is romantic novels and biographies of famous men. She wanted me to find a two-room apartment and give parties and do my absolute graphics at night, as a hobby. She would always threaten me with the past or the future: her lovers and what each one had done with her or had in mind to do, or the chance she might go running home to her parents, who had a family tree that went back seven hundred years and proved that one of her forefathers was chamberlain to the Pope. But what good was all that when we would go through all my two-week pay check in a couple of days? We'd scrape together some leftovers, or she'd return some bottles or rip up her clothes and sell them for rags. You've got to hand it to her. It was our only income for a while."

Two policemen came up to the glass door.

"Well, it's about time," said the tap woman as the policemen stamped the water out of their boots. "Those bug-eyed nuts out there are turning this place into a first-rate side show." She pointed to the onlookers, who had now quieted down, their eyes glittering with anticipation. "They'll drive me out of my mind yet. What kind of people get their kicks out of watching people hang themselves?"

She looked up startled at the younger of the two policemen. "What's the matter? Get into an argument or something?" The policeman took out a pocket mirror, examined his black eye, and said, "She got me with her shoe."

"What did I tell you?" said his superior. "Never get mixed up with a drunken wedding. One thing led to another, and our young friend here finally convinced the bridegroom to give him that handsome shiner."

"Ah, but I took care of him. He's behind bars until morning." He ran his finger around his eye again.

"All right, now, where's the girl?" asked the older policeman.

"In here," said the tap woman, drawing the curtain. The glass front of the cafeteria was covered with white hands, and the people in the second row were trying to push away the people up front. Several of the onlookers looked as if they were hanging from street lights, and one old man stood in the crown of the tree like a baboon, and the wind whipped up the rain like a set of draperies.

The young policeman took out his pad and inserted a piece of carbon paper.

Walking up and down the front window, the tap woman sneaked in a quick spit at the face of one of the onlookers, but the man never blinked an eye, and the spittle ran down the window like a milky tear.

"What is this, anyway? Do you think I beat my father to death with a chain?" she called out to them, and punched another one in the face. Then, in a rage, she undid her apron and covered over the tap. She let down her long hair—it was done up in a beehive—stuck the bobby pins in her mouth, and then began recoiling it in all its serpentine glory. When every strand was back in place she went into the alcove and sat down.

"Glad you're back," said the older policeman. "Unbutton her blouse, will you? She's got no papers on her at all. Just some small change." The bride had come up to the glass door and was tapping on it contritely. The young man let her in.

She took off a silver slipper and poured out the water. Her bridal wreath was in total disarray, and her eye make-up was streaking down her face.

"Well, what do you say?" she said. "Are you going to turn him loose or aren't you?"

"He stays where he is," said the policeman.

"But why?"

"Because he was disrespectful to a police officer in the line of duty."

"But it hardly even shows," she said, bending down to take a drink from the faucet, which was still dripping into the sink.

"My eye is as black as a piece of carbon paper," said the policeman, looking into his round pocket mirror.

"Well, you should have let us alone. You started it. Now finish it. When are you going to let him out?"

"Tomorrow."

"Well then, I'll just wait here for you, and you can come sleep with me. I don't want to be alone on my wedding night."

"You're not my type," said the policeman, getting up.

"Well, you're not the only one here," she said, waltzing around to the young man. "What about you?" she asked him. "How do *you* like me?"

"Oh, very much," he answered. "You're just like the girl who ran out on me. Your eyes look just the way hers did when she came down to my cellar apartment that first time. All she had with her was the kind of suitcase little girls carry around for their dolls. She was nearly barefoot, too; all she had on her feet was a pair of scrubby old shoes with perforated tongues. And her hair was cut real short, the way they wear it at reform school. You've got blue spots in your eyes, like a chip of chalcedony. You know, I really like you. You're just my type."

"Well, I like you too," said the bride. She filled her silver slipper with water, picked it up by its glass heel, and took a deep drink. "To each his own," she said, smacking her lips.

The young policeman took a seat, while his superior pulled back the curtains and dictated.

"The unidentified victim is slightly less than five foot three and is wearing a yellow and red plaid suit, black shoes with perforated tongues, and a pink blouse with a lace collar decorated with roses . . ."

The young policeman got up to close the door left open by the young man and the bride, who had just stepped out into the ribbons of the evening downpour. Back in his seat, he resumed his stenographic duties to the sergeant's dictation. Finally the ambulance from the morgue arrived with the pathologist.

"When my girl came to stay with me that first time . . ." said the young man.

"I can't hear you!" yelled the bride, the wind whipping the words out of her mouth.

"My girl," he yelled into her ear, "when she first came to stay with me, I was just finishing off a death mask for a friend. Well, she asked me to make one for her too, so she could start a new life. So I lay her down on the table and smeared her with Vaseline and stuck newspaper cones up each of her nostrils, and then I poured liquid plaster over her face— there was a towel around her neck as if she had just been strangled—and held her hand and felt the seismographic record of her heart."

"Gosh, that's beautiful!" cried the bride as the wind stripped her of her wreath, whisking it off through the pitch-black sky.

The young man stopped and looked over at a small park lit up by yellow street lights. A gust of wind had torn some young poplars from their supports and bent them over so far that their branches were dragging in the puddles.

"Grab hold of that tree," he called to her. He tore his tie in two and tied the sapling firmly to its pole.

"How come you make such a fuss over those trees?" she yelled.

"Don't let go!"

"I said, 'Why do you make such a fuss over the trees?'"

"They might fall down."

"Well, let them. What do you care?"

"These trees are public property, just like everything I say and do. You know, I'm as public as a public pissoir or a public park."

And so saying, he tore off the bride's wet and mud-splotched train, and with the powerful grace of an orchestra conductor he tore the silk into strips, which he then twisted into long cords.

"And when the plaster dried," he shouted, "the only way I could think of to get her free was to chisel her out. And in the process I had to cut half her hair off. That brought us together. Then she told me that the death mask marked the start of a new life for her, so for three days straight she confessed her sins to me. I would have knocked my head clean through the wall by the time she was done if I hadn't luckily had a supply on hand a supply of tar for insulating cellar walls. So I performed my father confessor role by brushing that tar over the white wall under the influence of her confessions: how they used to carry her to the bathroom when she had to throw up and how when a lover once abandoned her she lay outside all night and ate dirt to ease the pain. Well, by the time she'd confessed all her blackest sins and was lily white again, I had smeared an entire barrel of black tar over the white cellar wall. Say, do you have something else there I could tear off? I've run out of cord."

"Tear off whatever you like," she said, offering him a shoulder.

And with one mighty heave—like a branch cracking or the tram conductor pulling his bell rope—with one mighty yank, he tore the rest of her wedding gown off.

A flash of lightning struck, and there she stood, half naked in the public park.

"Hey," she said, "how about doing a death mask of me?"

WANT TO SEE GOLDEN PRAGUE?

Mr. Bamba, the little undertaker, walked down to the river on his way back from town. He followed the river in the direction of the oak grove.

"Mr. Bamba!" He turned around.

"Well, well, well. Mr. Kytka!" said Mr. Bamba. "What are you doing down here by the water? Looking for inspiration?"

"As a matter of fact," said Mr. Kytka, "I was just on my way from your place. Could you give me a little of your time?"

"I always have time for a poet," said Mr. Bamba.

"Well, our Surrealist Circle was wondering if you could lend us your establishment for an evening."

"You mean you want to set up a cabaret in my coffin ware-house?"

"No taxiaret, Mr. Bamba. Nothing as ordinary as that. We've got Breton and Eluard behind us, and our own beloved Karel Hynek Mácha too."

"What else?"

"In honor of the anniversary of Mácha's death, Jan z Woj-kowic is going to give a lecture."

"Jan z Wojkowic? Why, he's been confined to his bed for twenty years!"

"That's why I came looking for you, Mr. Bamba," said the poet. "I wanted to tell you that we are planning to transport the ancient bard to your coffin-making establishment bed and all."

"Sounds like a good time," said Mr. Bamba.

"Quite right," replied Mr. Kytka, looking across a stone wall to where two young bulls were grazing.

"There'll be photographers too, I suppose," said Mr. Bamba, standing on his toes.

"Right again. And all the pornographs will go straight into the hands of André Breton. . . . Those cows must be as strong as an ox."

"Where?" asked Mr. Bamba, standing on his toes.

"Here, let me hoist you up."

The undertaker lifted his arms like feather dusters, and the enormous poet had no trouble picking him up.

"Those are bulls, not oxen," declared Mr. Bamba when he had had his fill of the sight on the other side of the stone wall.

"Shall I put you down?"

"Yes, please," said Mr. Bamba. "Do you think your old poet friend will be willing to give that lecture?" he asked once they were on their way again. "I thought he only believed in mental telepathy."

"It's all set," said the poet. "My latest sex object, that beautiful young lady who works at the post office, has been having chest trouble lately, and he's been giving her the massage treatment. It was during one of the treatments that she got him to agree to the lecture."

"Are you making fun of me, Mr. Kytka? Are you pulling my leg?"

"Now what would I be wanting with your lower limb?"

"Okay, I believe you."

On the other side of the river the local fire brigade was going through maneuvers. Their helmets gleamed, catching and reflecting the rays of the sun. Two men were kneeling over the fire engine, while a third held the nozzle of the hose, his legs spread wide apart, in anticipation of the kick from the high-pressure stream of water. The bugler stood poised with one hand resting on his hip and the other pressing the bugle to his lips. Watching the brigade commander out of the corner of his eye, he finally got his signal and blew his piece, but not a drop emerged from the hose.

"They must have a stopped-up libido," said the poet.

"But I keep my coffins in the cellar. The coal is up on the second floor," said Mr. Bamba.

"All the more paranoid," said Mr. Kytka happily, and he turned around and yelled out across the river, "Hope you get your pump working!"

"Why, you dirty son of a Jordanian cow! You just worry about your own," yelled back the man holding the hose.

"Do you think we'll be able to get that bed down my stairs?" asked Mr. Bamba nervously. "And what if it rains? Wouldn't it be a good idea to load the poet and his bed into my hearse and ride along the arcade? Then the old guy could knock on the windows and bow to the people as we drove along."

"Quite right," said the poet. "Positively schizophrenic. What a mind you have there, Mr. Bamba! How about dropping by our Surrealist Circle sometime?"

"Oh no, thanks," said Mr. Bamba modestly. "I'm already a member of the Society for the Improvement of Parks and Playgrounds."

"I see. . . . Now the main thing is that we have enough black velvet hangings. You know, the kind you use to spruce up the catafalques. We want to decorate your cellar with them."

"Good choice. You barely touch the stuff and the dearly departed come tumbling out."

"Quite right. Say, what would you think about having invitations to the lecture printed up on those purple funeral ribbons?" asked the poet, and yelled, "Hope you get your pump working!" across the river.

"Why, you dirty son of a Jordanian cow! You want a smack in the mouth?" the firemen yelled back at him, running knee-deep into the river and shaking their fists.

"So there'll be pictures of my coffin room hanging in Paris," said the undertaker proudly.

"That's right," said the poet. "We surrealists"—and he pointed to himself—"are an international movement. We've got style. We lie at the feet of the sphinx." Then he turned around and yelled, "Hope you get it working!" across the water.

The firemen stopped fiddling with the engine, ran knee-deep into the river after their chief, and brandishing their screw-drivers and monkey wrenches, screamed out, "Why, you dirty son of a Bamba! You want a quick swim in the Elbe?"

"But I didn't say anything," Mr. Bamba yelled back, un-nerved.

"Next time you march in a funeral procession, we'll crack the crucifix right over your skull," barked the fire chief.

"Now look what you've done," said Mr. Bamba with a frown. "Think of all the firemen who will take their business to my competitor. And firemen go in for fancy funerals!"

"Watch me give them something to live for," said the poet and, cupping his hands around his mouth, he called out, "I'm the one who said it. Me. Kytka."

"So it was you, Kytka, you dirty bastard," roared the captain. "Just you wait. You'll get yours too."

Mr. Bamba rubbed his hands with pleasure.

"Mr. Kytka, you're not only a poet, you're a man with character. Hey, how about borrowing that white angel from the pharmacy and hanging it in the coffin room above the bed? Or how about asking the watchmaker to lend us the big clock he has hanging in front of his store, and installing it over the head of the old poet when he gives his lecture? Wouldn't it be a nice touch, the second hand as big as my leg ticking away the evening . . ."

Mr. Bamba stopped to catch his breath, and the poet swallowed hard.

"Mr. Bamba," he said after a while, "you have a double maniacal delta flowing through you. For weeks now I've been pecking around for ideas, and you just pick them out of your hat." Then Mr. Kytka raised his eyes to the sky and said, "This man"—pointing to the undertaker—"this man, not I, is a poet."

"Now you're overdoing it," said Mr. Bamba modestly.

"Not at all," said the poet. "Of course: the heathen, ignorant of faith, stumble upon the truth. Well now, Mr. Bamba. Is everything set?" He put out an enormous hand.

"You bet," said Mr. Bamba, and put his dainty little hand into the poet's paw.

Then Mr. Kytka took out his watch. "There!" he said, and pulled a batch of picture postcards from his breast pocket. "In a little while I'll be taking these views to the mail car of the Prague express. The local postmaster has forbidden them to travel by ordinary channels. He claims they're pornography."

Mr. Bamba opened the postcards into a fan and slapped his palm to his forehead. "How in the world do you make them?"

"I cut up my mother's marriage manual, a catalogue of ladies' undergarments, and finally the family Bible," said the poet, putting up his hand to stop the undertaker from interrupting. "Then I find some out-of-the-way place, free-associate myself into a trance, and paste the mixed clippings onto art nouveau pictures of naked women."

"How do they react in the mail car?"

"The reaction was the same yesterday as the day before, and I don't expect anything different today. I stick the cards through a crack in the wall of the mail car and pound on the door. The official takes the cards and postmarks them. I step down onto the tracks and watch him slapping his forehead and telling the man working with him to drop everything and come take a look. Then the two of them go through the cards, slapping their foreheads. Then the one with the green rubber visor goes up to the engineer, who wipes off his hands with cellulose, looks through the cards, and then slaps his forehead like the others. You can't imagine how attractive surrealistic objects can be, Mr. Bamba!"

"Yes, but I'm a member of the Society for the Improvement of Parks and Playgrounds," said Mr. Bamba in his own defense. "By the way, who do you send them to?"

"Beautiful young ladies who wish to throw off the bonds of sexual hypocrisy," said the poet, and then added prophetically, "because reality is alcoholic."

"Quite right," said Mr. Bamba, looking up at him. "But you know, when you lifted me up to see those two young bulls, I remembered having heard about a maid who once showed Golden Prague to the little boy she was looking after, and when she set him back down on the floor he keeled over dead. Have you ever heard about that?"

"Never," said the poet, brightening up.

"Well, that wasn't the end of it. The high point came in court when the judge screamed, 'How could you let a thing like that happen?' So the maid, who was as much of a giant as you, asked the tiny judge, 'Want to see Golden Prague?' and the judge said, 'I do,' and she took the judge's head between her palms and lifted him up to the ceiling. And when she put that judge down, he keeled over dead too!"

"Surreal!" Mr. Kytka exclaimed and, lifting his eyes to heaven, he lamented, "Here I've been pecking around the highways and byways for it, and he"—and he pointed to the owner of the funeral parlor—"he just picks it out of his hat!"

"Mr. Kytka," said Mr. Bamba with growing emotion, "I can't sleep at night when I think about it. My father used to show me the beauties of Prague all the time, and nothing ever happened to me. Could it be that people are more fragile nowadays? What do you say? Why don't we have a go at it?"

"But you could never get me off the ground," said the poet.

"No, *you* pick *me* up. I'm just an infant compared to you."

The motor on the other side of the water had begun to hum. The bugler raised his golden bugle back to his lips, and a fireman grasped the golden nozzle and steadied himself to prevent himself from being thrown off balance by the pressure. All the firemen's helmets glistened in the sun like gold. The fire chief gave the signal, the bugle rasped out over the meadows, and out of the hose shot a mighty stream that pitched the fireman with the nozzle back and forth.

"Now what do you say?" yelled the commander with a theatrical gesture in the direction of the stream, which by this time was arching through the air and landing in the middle of the river. "Working fine, isn't it?"

"Now, sure," yelled back the poet, "but what about that time a few weeks ago . . ."

"Why, you dirty son of a Jordanian cow! Just wait until I get you alone someday," cried the commander and, unbuttoning the ax from his belt, he ran into the water. The two firemen who had been kneeling by the engine followed suit, and in the end every one of them was threatening Kytka with a golden ax that caught and reflected the rays of the sun. "We'll knock your block off!"

"I'm just an infant compared to you," said Mr. Bamba as a reminder. His eyes were gleaming.

"Want to see Golden Prague?" asked the poet.

"I do," said Mr. Bamba, closing his eyes.

LOVING AND GIVING

Molly Keane

In 1904, when Nicandra is eight, all is well in the big Irish house called Deer Forest. Maman is beautiful and adored. Dada, silent and small, mooches contentedly around the stables. Aunt Tossie, of the giant heart and bosom, is widowed but looks splendid in weeds. The butler, the groom, the land-steward, the maids, the men – each has a place and knows it. Then, astonishingly, the perfect surface is shattered; Maman does something too dreadful ever to be spoken of.

'What next? Who to love?' asks Nicandra. And through her growing up and marriage her answer is to swamp those around her with kindness – while gradually the great house crumbles under a weight of manners and misunderstanding.

Also by Molly Keane in Abacus:

GOOD BEHAVIOUR

TIME AFTER TIME

0 3491 0088 8
ABACUS FICTION £3.99

WONDERFUL YEARS, WONDERFUL YEARS

George V. Higgins

'A likeable, crooked Massachusetts contractor sends his sedated schizophrenic wife to a derelict hotel in the Berkshires to muffle her before the hearing; his chauffeur prudently clobbers a vicious drunk in the car park, whereby hangs a long tale; a political thruster hopes to clinch a top appointment with a successful prosecution if someone can be pressured into talking. The Higgins dialogue adds its own special grit and magic to a carousel of the good, the bad, and the sexually careless' *Observer*

'A must . . . Philip Marlowe would have loved it' *Time Out*

'The new George V. Higgins novel, like all the old ones, is set in Boston. With more authority than any of his contemporaries, Mr Higgins can show us how to scratch that city and watch the corruption start to glimmer underneath' *Independent*

Also by George V. Higgins in Abacus:

OUTLAWS
IMPOSTERS
PENANCE FOR JERRY KENNEDY
KENNEDY FOR THE DEFENSE

0 3491 0075 6
ABACUS FICTION £3.99

BETTY BLUE

Philippe Djian

The major European bestseller that was made into the
celebrated film.

'A brilliant, painful account of a doomed love affair. While the
storm clouds are gathering, the teller of the story believes the
picnic is forever. Much, much better than the film' *Carlo Gébler*

'A powerful, picaresque tale of a relationship which moves into
the frenetic and finally the tragic' *Yorkshire Post*

'A simple story of love found and thwarted that also becomes a
remarkable journey backward: from modernist narrative
resignation and ennui into full-fledged emotional engagement,
complication, deepening of character and resolution . . . The
transformation of character is powerful, convincing, reverberant;
the love story is sad and fine' *Kirkus Reviews*

'Djian is a major writer. A page of his prose reads like nothing
else, except perhaps another page of his. His writing is the real
thing' *Le Monde*

'An atmosphere reminiscent of, by turns, *Diva* and *Paris, Texas*
. . . Djian's books soar above those of his contemporaries' *Paris
Match*

0 3491 0110 8
ABACUS FICTION £4.50

<u>DELIVERANCE</u>

James Dickey

Four men set out from a small Southern town for a three-day camping and canoe trip . . . a holiday jaunt that turns into a nightmare struggle for survival.

This is much more than a terrifying story of violence – murderous violence, sexual violence, and the violence of nature – it is a brilliant study of human beings driven towards – and sometimes beyond – the limits of endurance.

Shattering, spellbinding, and a masterly piece of writing, *Deliverance* has been described as the classic novel of male conflict and survival.

'A novel that will curl your toes . . . the limit of dramatic tension' *New York Times*

'A brilliant tale of action' *Observer*

'A fast, shapely adventure tale' *Time Magazine*

'Brilliant and breathtaking' *New Yorker*

0 3491 0076 4
ABACUS FICTION £3.99

GRACE

Maggie Gee

Grace is eighty-five, was once loved by a major painter, and now deplores the modern evils that rampage across the world. To escape the tyranny of silent phone calls that plague her, she goes to the seaside. To Seabourne where nothing ever happens except quiet deaths and holidays. Paula is her niece. Also a victim of mysterious harassment, she lives near the railway line that carries nuclear waste through the heart of London. She feels curiously, constantly unwell. Bruno is a sexually quirky private detective who attacks daisies with scissors, germs with bleach, and old ladies for fun.

A novel of towering stature, with all the stealth and suspense of a thriller, *Grace* is written in condemnation of violence and secrecy, in praise of courage and the redeeming power of love.

'*Full of poignancy and power*'
JEANETTE WINTERSON

'*Heart-stoppingly exciting*'
TIME OUT

'*Controlled and highly imaginative . . . this exceptional novel should be read everywhere*'
LITERARY REVIEW

'*Magically, I finished this book with the almost cheerful feeling that things are still hopeful as long as people answer back and write as well as this*'

GUARDIAN

0 349 10103 5   FICTION

A
CAPOTE
READER

A Capote Reader contains virtually all of the author's published work –
including several short pieces that have never before been published in book
form. It is divided into six parts: *Short Stories* (twelve of them, all that Capote
ever wrote); two *Novellas*, *The Glass Harp* and *Breakfast at Tiffany's*; *Travel
Sketches* (thirteen of them, mostly around the Mediterranean); *Reportage*,
including the famous Porgy and Bess trip to Russia *The Muses Are Heard*, and
the bizarre murders in *Handcarved Coffins*; *Portraits* of the famous, among
them Picasso, Mae West, Isak Dinesen, Chaplin, André Gide, Elizabeth
Taylor – who radiated 'a hectic allure' – and 'the beautiful child' Marilyn
Monroe; and *Essays* (seventeen of them, including *A Day's Work*). Each
section is in chronological order of publication, demonstrating the evolution of
the author's style and interests.

Also by Truman Capote in Abacus:
ANSWERED PRAYERS
MUSIC FOR CHAMELEONS
IN COLD BLOOD
BREAKFAST AT TIFFANY'S

0 3491 0095 0   FICTION

Abacus now offers an exciting range of quality fiction and non-fiction by both established and new authors. All of the books in this series are available from good bookshops, or can be ordered from the following address:

Sphere Books
Cash Sales Department
P.O. Box 11
Falmouth
Cornwall TR10 9EN.

Please send cheque or postal order (no currency), and allow 60p for postage and packing for the first book plus 25p for the second book and 15p for each additional book ordered up to a maximum charge of £1.90 in U.K.

B.F.P.O. customers please allow 60p for the first book, 25p for the second book plus 15p per copy for the next 7 books, thereafter 9p per book.

Overseas customers including Eire please allow £1.25 for postage and packing for the first book, 75p for the second book and 28p for each subsequent title ordered.